RIGHTEOUSNESS

Rajeshwar Prasad

TSL Publications

Dedication

Jagdip Mahto, my father and maker-like Thee,
For me the all who spread virtues over me –
Saying to follow only Truth rather than devils –
And for love and Ahimsa, stay away from evils.

Acknowledgement

Ella Walters for her assistance in editing the text.

Preface

True morality consists not in following the beaten track, but in finding out the true path for ourselves and in fearlessly following it.
M.K. Gandhi, *The Mind of Mahatma Gandhi*, p425

Man is a transitional being, evolving through the ages to become what he is today. However, the current evolutionary crisis signals a pivotal moment where he can transcend and embrace a higher destiny awaiting him. Created in the image of God, man carries hidden sparks of divinity within him, yet often remains unaware of his true potential. The ailments of worldly existence can be healed if man turns towards God and seeks the divine path on Earth.

Naturally, man is a rational being. Although not flawless, he stands as the most perfected among all creatures, endowed with the most evolved mind and body. It is incumbent upon him to recognize the challenges presented by the world. Instead of following the transient and changeable desires of the mortal body, he should heed the sacred voice of his inner spirit. His priority should be spiritual growth and advancement. By doing so, a powerful current of love and brotherhood will flow omnipotently throughout the world.

Society itself wields significant influence. If it acknowledges the world's challenges, it can effectively combat its vices. However, it's deeply troubling that contemporary social values are diminishing, with individuals undermining society and its principles to varying extents.

Living in today's world is immensely challenging, with no fixed formula that universally applies to human existence. Despite this, we must retain our faith in life. Truth remains immutable; nothing can conceal it in this world.

We all witness a person arriving here once, entitled to a life of minimal necessities and happiness. Sadly, many individuals prevent numerous others from living joyfully, subjecting them to continual suffering. The protagonist of this narrative falls victim to the same societal injustice.

All faiths profess equality, and we all assert knowledge of our respective religions. Yet, upon closer examination, many adherents confine their moral and ethical compasses under the guise of religion. Primarily, we must embody humanity before identifying with any religion. Without adhering to the religion of humanity, how can we rightfully claim allegiance to any specific faith?

There is no place for suppression, exploitation, violence, or atrocity in any civilised society. One should condemn these acts and consider aiding those in need as the noblest religion to practise in life, the true path to God. Remember figures like Mother Teresa, Mahatma Gandhi, and many others who sacrificed their lives for humanity and Mother Earth, their names etched in history, never to be forgotten.

The world is indeed a marvel of beauty, adorned with diverse shapes and colours. No one wishes to depart from this enchanting realm, and it is our collective duty to enhance its beauty rather than cast shadows upon it. This responsibility falls naturally upon every man and woman who enters this world.

This fictional work does not aim to criticise any caste, colour, community, race, religion, profession, society, country, or people. Instead, it venerates them all, anticipating that they will contribute to the world's magical beauty and provide humanity with a virtuous environment to thrive in. The work vehemently opposes exploitation, suppression, injustice, and atrocity. It also denounces conversions motivated by greed, fear, or coercion, as these spawn additional evils and erode social harmony. The work maintains steadfast faith in the rule of law and justice.

We possess a rich storytelling tradition handed down by our grandparents, imparting wisdom through generations. This tradition must endure for the betterment of humankind. While this book may not strictly adhere to that tradition, it reveals my personal experiences. I do not claim it harbours groundbreaking ideas; every word is an echo of old truths. It is the revelation of my inner spirit, penned with blood and tears.

Rajeshwar Prasad

Introduction

Life for some is straightforward but for the majority, I think, life comes with its ups and downs, including struggles and difficult times.

It has been interesting to read this book which is set in India: an amazing country I have travelled to and seen through the eyes of a tourist. The book, however, opened my eyes to new experiences, both bad and good as I read about the life of Ella, his family, community, and adversaries.

I immediately admired Ella, a 49-year-old man, and his genuine acceptance of his difficult, poverty-stricken life. He and his gentle wife Emily live in a mud-walled home with their children. They both have various jobs to scrape together enough money to survive and are well respected by their community.

As well as the story narrative, explanations about the way of life, details of what is 'normal' behaviour in the community, and reasons for this are included. This helps the reader understand more clearly the actions and inactions of the various characters. As I read, I found myself asking, 'What would I do if I was one of the characters?' 'Would I follow the crowd?' 'Would I be prepared to verbalize what was on my mind and face the consequences?'

Ella's religious faith shines through because he takes it seriously. While reading, I realised the novel is multi-layered. I found myself thinking not only about the plight of Ella but also about the book of Job in the Old Testament of the Christian Bible. Job also faced difficulties in his life so correlations can be seen between Ella and Job.

It is interesting to read about a different way of life in a different country to my own. And yet, parallels can be seen in how people are treated, and, sadly, mistreated in my country and throughout the world. Disappointingly, I am also aware in the UK of situations in which people in authority, the police, the legal system, and the media don't always get things right resulting in unfortunate outcomes.

This book is written in a different style and very different subject matter to my writing, but I found it to be a thought-provoking tale of contrasts; rich and poor, honest and dishonest, good and evil, right and wrong. Social discrimination and exploitation of the poor are evident too. I can't deny I found it uncomfortable and disturbing to read in parts and yet I wanted to find out how the story ended, so persevered.

Margaret L Moore
Author of *From Sri Lanka with love; a tapestry of travel tales*

CONTENTS

One of the Wonders

Ella stood apart from everyone else in the entire village. Integrity was paramount in his life, above everything. He held the belief that a life devoid of values held no purpose.

To Ella, virtue nourished the soul, morality adorned his character, honesty guided his actions, righteousness defined his conduct, and service to others constituted his religion. While he adhered to the same faith as his fellow villagers, he lived by different principles, with Truth as his guiding light.

Whenever the time came for Ella to act, he did so with righteousness, always glorifying God in his discussions. He consistently encouraged people to turn towards God, demonstrating a readiness to sacrifice everything for these principles – willing to shed his last drop of blood and breathe his final breath. However, his fellow villagers did not share the same perspective. They embraced life's pleasures, viewing existence without enjoyment as futile. Their focus was on material gains, pursuing activities solely for personal gain and neglecting moral virtues.

Ella resided in Vellore, distinctly different from all others in the village. While the village and its inhabitants were affluent, Ella lived in poverty. Despite his circumstances, he found contentment with what he possessed, appearing to be the most fulfilled person in the village.

Although economically poor, Ella was spiritually wealthy. He practised what he said, steadfastly adhering to virtues throughout his entire life. While many villagers succumbed to immoral paths, others advised Ella to follow suit. However, he remained resolute, steadfast in poverty yet unwavering in his commitment to truth, morality, and honesty. While others pursued happiness through any means, Ella found satisfaction in what he rightfully earned. He believed that practising love, truth, honesty, and nonviolence equated to worshipping God. Whenever he encountered suffering beings, he dedicated himself to their service.

He professed, "God resides within the soul of every being, and serving any creature is akin to serving God."

Service defined his beliefs. It was not just a practice but his religion, upheld throughout his life to the best of his ability.

Despite his humble means, Ella owned only a small plot of inherited land where he cultivated vegetables. His home, constructed from earthen materials, was modest yet brought him immense joy as he shared it with his family.

He often remarked, "Blessed is the person who owns a few acres of ancestral land. My humble earthen home is my paradise."

Ella possessed a small piece of land that caught the attention of several wealthy and influential villagers due to its prime location by the main road. They urged him to sell it, but he adamantly refused, stating he could not part with his paternal inheritance. Despite the challenges he faced in life, Ella remained steadfast in his principles, continuing to cultivate vegetables on a portion of his land and selling them in the nearby market to sustain himself.

Emily, his wife, was gentle and industrious. She assisted her husband in their agricultural endeavours and also took on part-time work as a maid for a wealthy villager. This additional income helped support their family alongside Ella's earnings from farming. Together, they managed to make ends meet and uphold their modest lifestyle despite the pressures and temptations around them.

Ella was renowned in the village for his unwavering determination and impeccable integrity. His reputation was built on never causing harm or offence to anyone, earning him universal respect and admiration.

During the rainy season, when agricultural activities thrived in the village, Ella secured additional work in the fields of his fellow villagers. This supplementary income bolstered his resources. Moreover, he possessed a talent for confectionery and was proficient in crafting various types of sweets. During wedding seasons, he undertook contracts to prepare sweets for his clients, leveraging his expertise to further support his livelihood.

Ella, a gentleman of forty-nine, resided in a mud-built house with two rooms. His wife Emily, slender and frail, bore four children: Leo, Luca, Levi, and Luke. Each morning, Emily would leave home with Levi and Luke, still young, to work at Ray's house. Her tasks included cleaning kitchen utensils and clothes, and in return, she received stale rice or chapatti, which brought her immense happiness to share with her children upon returning home late at night.

Despite their modest means, the family lived contentedly within their circumstances, fully participating in the societal currents and enjoying festivals such as Holi, Dussehra, and Diwali. Ella dressed in a dhoti like other men of the village, while Emily wore a sari like the local women. Their children donned pantaloons and shirts like their peers, albeit in more affordable attire than their counterparts.

Ella owned a small piece of land with a mud-built well, a valuable plot due to its strategic location where multiple roads intersected. Its roadside position made it highly sought after, despite its small size, as Ella had cultivated vegetables on it for years. This plot was not only his ancestral inheritance but also a vital source of livelihood.

Unexpectedly, a dramatic turn of events unfolded in Ella's life, causing a stir throughout the village. Harris, a sitting Member of Parliament from the Cester Parliamentary Constituency, illegally seized Ella's land. Ella was devastated and deprived of joy because his cherished piece of land had been forcefully taken from him. When Ella contested the seizure, Harris presented a sale deed supposedly signed by Ella's father, indicating the transfer of ownership. Ella vehemently objected, asserting that his father had never sold the land to anyone. He felt deeply aggrieved by this injustice and struggled to cope upon seeing the disputed sale deed.

Despite his distress, Ella insisted, "My father never sold it to anyone." His anguish and disbelief were palpable as he confronted the harsh reality of losing his ancestral land under dubious circumstances.

Harris remained unmoved by Ella's protests, showing no compassion. Instead, he insisted that Ella should simply accept the situation, asserting that Ella's father had sold the land out of financial necessity for fifty thousand rupees.

According to Harris, he had allowed Ella to use the land for eleven years solely out of goodwill, enabling Ella to earn a livelihood. Harris made it clear that he viewed his actions as anything but a gesture of mercy towards Ella, suggesting that without Harris's intervention, Ella would face dire consequences, possibly even eternal damnation.

Throughout Harris's assertions, Ella listened attentively and silently. He adamantly refuted Harris's claims, maintaining that his father had never sold the land to anyone. Despite Harris's firm stance, Ella remained resolute in his belief and refused to accept the unjust seizure of his ancestral property.

Ella fervently insisted that his father had never sold the land to Harris or anyone else in his lifetime. He pleaded with Harris not to seize the land, emphasizing its significance as his sole possession – a cherished symbol and blessing from his ancestors, vital for his livelihood. Ella went as far as to say he would rather forfeit his life than lose the land, knowing that without it, he and his children would face destitution.

The truth was clear: Ella's father had never authorized the sale of the land to Harris or anyone else. Unfortunately, in their area, numerous cases similar to Ella's were entangled in legal disputes, where influential individuals had acquired fraudulent sale deeds to usurp property from the unsuspecting poor. Such injustices often went unchecked for years, with the judicial process rarely favouring the disadvantaged unless under exceptional circumstances.

Ella's situation highlighted the harsh reality faced by many like him, where their rightful claims were overshadowed by deceit and exploitation. Despite Ella's earnest appeals and the truth of his father's ownership, the path to justice seemed fraught with obstacles, offering little hope for a fair resolution outside of extraordinary circumstances.

In the meantime, the condition of Ella was the same. Instead of showering mercy on him, Harris was agitated and warned him. He said that Ella was misguiding him and that his father had sold the said land. He said, "Ella, don't misguide me. Go away. Go away and never look behind. I am not a contractor of your life or your children's lives. Go to the abyss or befool someone else, not me. Otherwise, I will crush you with my fist."

Ella remained composed despite Harris's threats. Refusing to leave, he stayed put. Frustrated by Ella's defiance, Harris instructed his bodyguard to physically assault him. The bodyguard complied, attacking both Ella and Emily. The brutality of the assault caused Emily to lament loudly, pounding her chest like a drum, while Ella sat on the edge of the field, overcome with tears.

This traumatic incident plunged Ella and his entire family into a deep sea of suffering and hardship, robbing them of peace and tranquillity. The following morning, determined to seek justice, Ella took it upon himself to visit every household in the village, urging them to convene a community meeting to address the injustice inflicted upon him.

Ella spoke passionately to the villagers, asserting that his father had never sold any land to anyone, yet Harris had illegally and forcefully seized his property. He recounted how he and his wife were assaulted by Harris's bodyguard when they objected to the unjust occupation.

Despite Ella's plea for support and a social meeting to address the injustice, the villagers hesitated. Fear of Harris's influence loomed large; his power was so intimidating that merely casting a shadow of dissent against him seemed unthinkable. No one dared to defy him openly or speak out against his actions. Consequently, Ella found himself standing alone in his quest for justice, as the villagers remained silent and unwilling to confront Harris's authority.

The villagers expressed their reluctance to get involved, citing Harris's formidable influence and the potential consequences of opposing him. They warned Ella that any dissent against Harris could lead to personal ruin, emphasizing that it was wiser to abandon the fight for his land and find contentment with what little he had. To them, calling a social meeting to confront Harris would only invite more trouble and sorrow into their lives.

This reluctance to challenge powerful figures is a common trait in such societies, where people prioritize their own interests and often see benefits in maintaining relationships with influential individuals who could provide assistance when needed. They even support such figures politically, despite their criminal backgrounds and legal troubles, viewing them as more effective in navigating the system. This dynamic creates an environment where individuals like Ella, seeking justice against powerful adversaries, find themselves isolated and without support.

Despite his efforts to rally community support, Ella faced insurmountable odds. The villagers' fear and self-interest outweighed any inclination to stand together against injustice, leaving Ella to confront his plight alone, without the solidarity he desperately sought.

Social discrimination indeed plays a significant role in perpetuating exploitation against the poor. In societies divided into distinct sections, it's common for people from lower classes to face exploitation, even within government offices. Despite existing laws intended to protect the disadvantaged, many individuals flout these regulations, actively opposing measures that benefit the underprivileged. The prevailing sentiment was that justice for Ella was an unattainable ideal in his society and country.

Consequently, no one stepped forward to support Ella. Despite their sympathies, most advised him to relinquish his claim to the land to avoid further trouble and opposition. Despite these discouragements, Ella persisted, visiting each villager's home in the hope of garnering support. He even waited for four hours at the Community Hall, holding a lantern to signify his readiness for the meeting against Harris's injustice. However, no one joined him.

Disheartened, Ella eventually left the Community Hall and returned home, where his wife Emily anxiously awaited news of any progress. As they reunited, they began to discuss their next steps in the face of overwhelming isolation and opposition.

"What happened?"

"Nothing!"

"But, why not?"

"God knows – only He knows. No one came."

He continued, "I waited there for four hours, but all in vain. No one came even to ask me what was lost by me."

Emily's sorrowful weeping deeply affected her children, who joined her in tears. Their cries echoed unanswered, emphasizing the perceived indifference of the wealthy towards the plight of the poor. The situation grew increasingly poignant and desperate.

With no other recourse, Ella decided to pursue the first course of action: seeking justice from the Headman. The following day, he approached the Headman of Vellore and recounted the entire ordeal in painstaking detail, hoping for a resolution to his grievance.

Ella pleaded desperately with the Headman, laying bare his distress: "Sir! Harris has unlawfully seized my land. How can we survive? I will perish, my children will perish. Please, sir, help us. You are our only hope! You can save us. You are our saviour!"

In response, the Headman dismissed Ella's plea, claiming he misunderstood the situation. He advised Ella to abandon his pursuit and forget about the land. The Headman argued that the land held little value for Ella, suggesting it was in poor condition with makeshift leaf-shed walls that were an eyesore for Vellore. With the land now taken by Harris, the Headman reasoned, Harris would likely develop a grand and attractive building that would enhance the village's reputation. Therefore, according to the Headman, Ella could continue working at Ray's home without any worries.

Disheartened and dismayed by the Headman's refusal to intervene, Ella found himself abandoned once again, without the assistance he desperately sought.

Ella's heartbreak and despair left him speechless, tears streaming down his face until his clothes were soaked. He stood there, appearing lifeless and numb, as if his very being had been drained of vitality, resembling a motionless wooden figure.

Witnessing Ella in such a state, the Headman's response was callous and unsympathetic. He scolded Ella, demanding that he stop weeping and leave, admonishing him that his grief was not only distressing for the Headman but for the entire village. The Headman justified his harsh stance by explaining that important visitors often visited him, and Ella's emotional display could potentially disrupt their composure.

Despite the Headman's rebuke, Ella remained silent and resolute, standing before him. The Headman regarded him with contempt, his eyes burning with anger like a lion eyeing its prey. It was evident to anyone witnessing Ella's plight that he was suffering deeply, but the societal norms and power dynamics prevented anyone from stepping forward to support him in seeking justice.

One of the striking aspects was that although everyone knew the facts, no one stated that Harris was wrong and Ella was right. All were in favour of Harris, and someone even responded positively to make Harris feel better.

They praised Harris wholeheartedly, affirming that he was completely right. They agreed that the poor must die and relieve this holy earth of their sins of poverty – they should not linger in this world.

Hearing such sentiments from the officers present, Harris's chest swelled with pride, and his pleasure became uncontrollable. He felt confident that they would support him in occupying Ella's land, viewing the act as a delightful game. He considered himself fortunate to have such recognition among the officers. Though some believed he lacked the virtues that define a true man, no one expressed their inner thoughts.

Meanwhile, Harris and the others overlooked the grace and power of time and fate. Amidst the revelry, a few people chanted lines from John Dryden's *Mac Flecknoe*:

> *All human things are subject to decay*
> *And, when fate summons, monarchs must obey.*

They said that the loss of life for the prey is a joy for the hunter. Similarly, Harris's evil deeds pleased him, while they plunged Ella into a sea of woes and sorrows. However, Harris was oblivious to the fact that time spares no one – its powerful hands eventually reach everyone, from kings to commoners. Despite this inevitable truth, Harris continued to freely engage in illegal and immoral acts using his influence, forcing Ella to suffer as a result.

Some people also discussed that truth suffers but is never lost. Citing various examples from scriptures and daily life, they firmly asserted that truth eventually eradicates all evil. They believed that one day Ella would win his case. However, no one was willing to step forward to help Ella or condemn Harris's wrongdoing. Now, Ella was isolated in the village. Very few people spoke to him, and those who did made an effort to avoid him.

No one wanted to meet him; they hid their faces to avoid any expectation of help from him.

The Burial and Birds

It is well acknowledged that tragedy never comes alone, and this proved true for Ella's family. On the one hand, Harris had seized his land; on the other, poverty had completely ensnared them. In this dire situation, disease struck Emily, and she was bedridden with typhoid. Helpless and unable to perform her duties at Ray's home or even in her own, her mud-built house and kitchen utensils became very dirty. Her clothes were filthy as well. There was no one to care for her or clean her home. With no food available, she was hungry, and her children were desperate for even a piece of stale chapatti, which no one was likely to offer them.

Ella had no money for either Emily's treatment or food. The crops from his field, which could have fed them, were no longer his. He hadn't eaten in four days, and his children were also starving, sitting around their mother's sickbed. Sometimes, they asked for chapatti with salt and mustard oil, but there was nothing to eat in their home.

Near their home stood a margosa tree with some ripened fruits. In desperation, Ella wanted to give these to his children to keep them alive. He gathered the fallen margosa fruits and gave them to his children.

He spoke to them very pathetically, explaining that he couldn't bring anything from anywhere because their mother was ill. He reassured them that once she recovered, she would make them rice and chapatti, and they would go with her to Ray's home where they would eat chapatti and rice together. He tried to convince them that the margosa fruit was not bitter, but rather sweet and very beneficial for their health. He explained that if they ate it, their bodies would remain free from wounds and their blood would be purified.

But despite all this, Leo, Luca, Levi, and Luke could not eat even a single margosa fruit and continued to weep. Emily listened to all this but had no option except to watch and suffer. She remained silent, tears streaming from her eyes as she witnessed the family's dire situation. After some time, her children approached her, still demanding rice and chapatti. Overwhelmed, she lost her temper and became angry. The situation had become unbearable for her, and she began to scold them.

She said slowly, "Oh, helpless boys! Go away and die! You are worsening my ailment. You are draining my soul. From where will I get all this for you? Can't you see that someone has cast a spell on us? We are surrounded by problems with no solution in sight. Tears and sorrows all around us."

With nothing to eat in Ella's home, and Emily unable to provide even a small portion of stale rice or chapatti for her children from Ray's home, they grew increasingly lean and thin. Ella was tormented by the thought of what had caused his suffering, leading to Harris seizing his land and Emily falling ill. He wondered if a terrible ghost haunted his home, plunging him into deep distress. Desperate for answers, he decided to consult a sorcerer to understand the cause of his suffering and find a solution.

The next morning, he set out for the village where the sorcerer lived. Upon meeting him, Ella pleaded for help to save his family from their distress. The sorcerer asked him to recount all the events that had befallen his family over the past week, and Ella narrated the entire ordeal.

The sorcerer listened to Ella quietly and with great interest. He knew the details of his plight. He explained that Ella's family was suffering from the presence of a malevolent ghost from the same village – the restless soul of a young Brahmin lady who had died from an electric shock. The sorcerer mentioned that this ghost wanders homes in search of his children to harm. He advised Ella to expel this malevolent spirit from his house if he wished to live peacefully and happily.

Time was entirely against Ella, and he was unaware of the challenges yet to come. However, he believed in the sorcerer's ability to resolve his tragedies due to his frequent misfortunes.

Upon learning that his family was suffering from the ghost's presence, Ella sat on the ground before the sorcerer and pleaded helplessly. He begged for their lives to be saved, convinced that no one else could help him in such a dire situation. He implored the sorcerer to protect them from the malevolent ghost, believing that the sorcerer was the only merciful person who could offer assistance. Ella felt that everyone else had turned their backs on him despite his pleas for help, but he trusted the sorcerer to be different and kind.

The sorcerer observed his mental state and pondered it deeply. Watching him, he smiled and nodded as he studied his face. Meanwhile, Ella remained silent, waiting for his response. The sorcerer weighed the pros and cons and decided he was willing to perform sorcery to protect Ella. Sensing an opportunity for gain, he was keen not to let it slip away. Thus, he granted his request.

He instructed Ella to procure the following items for the ritual to banish the ghost: a dhoti, a sari, a rooster, 1¼ kilograms of sandalwood chips, 1¼ metres of red cloth, 1¼ metres of black cloth, 1¼ kilograms of ghee, a packet of vermilion, eyewash, and five thousand and one rupees.

He instructed Ella to listen to him very seriously and carefully. He must perform the most crucial ritual of his entire life as soon as possible. If the ritual was not completed within a week, the ghost would kill every member of his family, leaving no one alive to even light a candle in their home. The ghost was now ravenous for the lives of men and women – particularly young men and infants.

Upon learning this, Ella departed for his home. The sorcerer had influenced Ella's mind so profoundly that he constantly felt and saw ghosts all around him in his house. He imagined ghosts sleeping beside him or sitting with him, creating a pitiable state for himself. Near his only calf, he even saw a deceptive ghost.

Desperate to be free from the ghosts haunting his house, he resolved to sell his only calf at any cost. Upon reaching his home, he untied the calf and quickly headed to the cattle fair. There, he aimed to sell it for six thousand rupees, but no one was willing to buy it at that price. As the day wore on, the setting sun cast a red beam on the calf, and he grew increasingly anxious. The day had nearly ended, and not a single customer had shown interest in buying the calf. His heart pounded with dread, knowing he had no other means to gather the money required for the ritual prescribed by the sorcerer.

Just then, a customer approached, showing interest in the calf. He began to negotiate with Ella.

"How much does the calf cost?"

"Six thousand rupees only," Ella replied.

The customer countered, "Will you sell the calf for three thousand rupees?"

"No! I have raised this red calf with my blood, so its price must be at least six thousand rupees. This strong calf is five years old. If you're willing to pay its true price, then you may buy it. Otherwise, leave."

Hearing this, the customer walked away. As the fair began to darken, people started to leave one by one until only a few remained. It seemed there was no chance of selling the calf. However, he was determined to sell it at any cost to buy the items required by the sorcerer.

After a few minutes, another customer approached him and asked, "How much does the calf cost?"

"Six thousand rupees only," he replied.

"It is evening. No one else will come to purchase it now. If you want to sell it, take one thousand rupees and sell it to me; otherwise, go back home. Are you ready? Tell me quickly."

He then added, "Take one thousand and five hundred rupees."

Ella remained silent, trapped in a dilemma. Ultimately, his right hand moved forward, and the customer placed the money into it. Accepting the amount, Ella sold the calf and went to the market to buy the items specified by the sorcerer. He purchased everything as instructed and tied it all into a bundle.

With the bundle, he went straight to the sorcerer to inform him. When he arrived, the sorcerer was smoking hemp. Seeing the heavy bundle on Ella's head, the sorcerer was very pleased.

"O Ella! Have you purchased everything? Did you miss anything?"

"Yes, Baba! I bought everything you told me to."

"All the items?"

"Yes, yes, Baba! Everything you mentioned!"

"Go back to your home. I will come soon after finishing my smoke."

On the same day, the sorcerer arrived at Ella's home at midnight and requested all the items needed to begin the ritual to banish the deceptive ghost. Ella handed over the items, and the sorcerer commenced his ghostly procedure, working for four hours. Finally, he gave Ella a mysterious object to tie to Emily's left arm with a red thread. He also instructed Ella to scatter ash along the path where the ritual had been performed, ensuring that someone would step on it in the morning.

The sorcerer then lightly struck Ella's wife and children with a leather shoe, proclaiming that the ghost had fled their home and had promised the sorcerer never to return.

At 4 a.m., when Ella went to scatter the ghostly ash along the way, the sorcerer wrapped up all the items in red cloths and left for his home.

Upon returning home after scattering the ash, Ella slept on a straw-made mat. However, as he slept, he heard the weeping of his children, who were sleeping beside their mother. Concerned, he went to them to inquire about the cause of their distress. To his dismay, he found Emily with fog in her throat, mist on her face, snow on her body, and blasts coming from her mouth. The god of death had visited her, and she was nearing the end of her life. Observing her condition, Ella understood the reason behind the fog, mist, and blasts.

So, he hurried to fetch water and cupped it in his right palm, gently dropping a few drops into her mouth. As he did so, she slipped into a sleep from which she would never awaken. She wouldn't see the sun after the sorcery had been performed.

Ella's situation now grew even more dire. He had no money to purchase even a shroud for Emily. Therefore, as the sun rose, he went from door to door, begging so that he could afford a shroud for her. From sunrise until 10 p.m., he begged and managed to collect only five hundred rupees. After finishing his rounds of begging, he returned home. However, it was too late at night to buy the shroud. The following morning, he went to Cester and purchased the shroud for Emily.

Villagers gathered, paying their respects and showing pity and sympathy for her. Emotions ran high, with some even shedding tears at the sight of her lifeless body.

The depiction of Emily's life and her departure reflects a deep sense of community and spirituality. Despite her gentle nature and willingness to serve, fate dealt her a harsh hand, plunging her and her family into poverty. This portrayal acknowledges the inevitability of fate, attributing it to a higher power. The community's prayers for peace and the soul's rest, coupled with the solemnity of the funeral rituals and the diverse participation in the funeral march, underline the reverence and respect for Emily and her journey.

As the bier was positioned at the crematorium, preparations for the pyre commenced. The bier, adorned in a fresh and gleaming shroud, captured the attention of onlookers, for they had seldom seen Emily so adorned.

This moment invoked an indelible memory: the day Emily arrived in Vellore as a radiant bride, welcomed warmly by the villagers. Now, for the second time, she was adorned in new attire, this time for her eternal departure from Vellore, bidding farewell amidst the gathered villagers. There seemed to be a poignant connection between the bridal procession of her arrival and the sombre funeral march of her departure.

When the pyre was ready, the people placed the body upon it. Ray, Ella's religious priest, stood at the head of the pyre and began to chant a holy mouth-fire hymn in Sanskrit. His chanting was devoid of accentuation, intonation, or pitch, and he recited the words in a rapid, monotone fashion characteristic of the priest's role. In the local language, his chant was as fast as a machine. As Ray chanted the holy mouth-fire hymn, Ella ignited the mouth of Emily's body with the holy fire. Thus, her body was dedicated to the sacred flames.

Meanwhile, the people circled the pyre five times, each time adding a piece of sacred wood to the fire. Within an hour, Emily's body was completely cremated, transforming into the five holy elements: earth, water, fire, sky, and air.

After the cremation, the people left the crematorium and headed home. Along the way, they discussed, "Whatever happens, happens for the best." They remarked that her death was preferable to suffering in poverty, where she struggled to obtain even a single meal, enduring each moment as if it were a prolonged agony. They felt that there was no difference between a moment of poverty and a century of affluence.

They offered Ella their condolences in various ways, appearing to be his well-wishers, despite never having supported him when Harris had illegally seized his land. They expressed their sympathy for him in different manners, saying that everyone has to leave this world eventually. They assured Ella that there was no need to be anxious about Emily's passing. Time would move on, and he would find a way to endure, whether he liked it or not, as he had to follow the will of fate.

In the meantime, he remained silent, following them slowly. People tried to justify the situation, saying, "She passed away only because of poverty – that poverty was a curse from an Unseen Power, not the fault of society." They suggested that fate had determined she would live in poverty, while others enjoyed affluence.

People remarked that Ella's circumstances were due to fate or perhaps a curse from God. They discussed the helplessness of man, insisting that society played no role in his suffering and placing the blame squarely on fate or divine will.

Around a hundred people had gathered, each reacting differently. Some spoke like philosophers, others like ordinary people – ideas varied widely. It seemed as if they had assembled to absolve anyone or anything from the great curse of the divine. Yet, they had never come together to save her from the cruel grasp of poverty, which was a direct result of that very society. They had gathered to bid farewell to her dead body on this occasion. It was clear that civilized society harboured enmity towards the living, not the dead. They had not come together to save her life, but now, in her death, they had wholeheartedly assembled to cremate her body.

Meanwhile, Ella found himself in a dilemma, torn between two conflicting emotions. On one hand, he felt a sense of relief that Emily's suffering had ended. On the other hand, he was overwhelmed by the social and religious rituals he was expected to perform after her death. His greatest problem was his lack of money to carry out these rituals.

Despite his dire financial situation, Ella was determined to perform the rituals at any cost, believing this would allow him to continue living in a civilized society. He felt an intense pressure to conform to social expectations, even if it meant borrowing money. However, he had no idea who might lend it to him. Despite being unable to provide even a square meal for himself and his sons, Ella's strong desire to perform these rituals was driven by the psychological pressure to fulfil his social obligations.

He decided to borrow money and planned to visit his relative's home the following morning. Gathering some ripe peepal fruits, he gave them to his children to eat. At dawn the next day, he set off to his relative's house to ask for financial help to perform the social and religious rituals for the late Emily. His relative agreed and lent him three thousand rupees.

That same day, having secured the money, Ella returned home. Upon arrival, he noticed that the peepal fruits he had left on a large banana leaf for his children were untouched. This sight troubled him, and without delay, he rushed to the room where his children were sleeping. Pulling back the straw sheet, he discovered that Levi and Luke were dead, and Leo and Luca were unconscious.

Seeing the lifeless bodies of his children, his heart turned to stone. His eyes could not shed a single tear of love or attachment. No words escaped his lips; he seemed mute. He sat there, silent and motionless, for an hour. Finally, he stood up and tied the dead bodies together with a string, like a bundle of sugarcane. Placing the bundle on his head and carrying a spade on his shoulder, he walked towards the Toss River.

Upon reaching the riverbank, he callously dropped the bundle onto the sand and began to dig a grave. As he dug, he used his feet to push the bundle of bodies into the hole, covering them with sand and stones from the riverbed.

The situation was too pathetic, quite intolerable for anyone. How was he enduring such a trial in his life? Only the Almighty could answer. Such a stone-hearted act had perhaps never before occurred on this earth: a father burying his children's bodies with his feet, not his hands. The earth witnessed it and recorded it in indelible ink in the eternal register of Nature.

"*O! Forester! O! Worldly Forester!* What has been lost? In that moment, there was no religious priest to chant holy hymns, nor anyone to help Ella with the burial. Yet, several birds perched on the nearby trees, singing holy and divine songs in an elegiac tone with full-throated ease:

What has been snatched? What has been lost?
What has been robbed? What has been turned?"

Blowing wind, "Worldly things have been lost.
And poverty has gained. The social system has won.
Tears have been snatched. Mercy has been stolen.
Rest has been robbed. Humanity has been turned."

This mysterious song was coming from the trees by the river. Ella lost in his thoughts, continued his work. After burying his children, he returned home.

Indeed, Ella's heart had turned to stone. Unbelievably, it seemed as if he were burying a bucket of soil. He had no passion, no feelings, and no desire to do anything. As he walked back, some people sitting in the Community Hall watched him like lions eyeing their prey. They discussed his mental state, noting how he had buried his children without performing any death rituals or informing anyone in the village.

They muttered that Ella must indeed be a great sinner to have lost Emily, Levi, and Luke within four days. They speculated he had committed some unknown crimes, for such suffering befell only those who offended God. Outwardly, he seemed like a gentleman, but inwardly, they believed he was a sinner. Scriptures, they said, all agreed that no one suffered in such a manner unless they had committed a grave crime against the divine. If they shared in his sins, they feared they would lose everything except woes and sorrows. They pondered this seriously, contemplating their next steps.

Ella, however, was oblivious to their discussion. Lost in his thoughts, he continued on the path that led to his home.

Mysterious Voices

There were three friends of Ella – Ethon, Gill, and Bond – who were aware of his current tragedies. They went to his home but found it empty. Determined to find him, they decided to ask around the village. Luckily, they bumped into Ella, one by one, as they ventured out.

Firstly, Ethan encountered him. A close friend who had shared in his joys and sorrows in the past.

"How are you, Ella? Where are you coming from?"

"You understand."

"What?"

"Everything is right in front of you."

"It's natural …"

With that, Ethan continued on his way, leaving Ella to ponder his own troubles and sorrows. Though emotional, he managed to keep his composure. Eventually, he resumed his journey home.

After a few minutes, Gill, his second friend, crossed paths with him.

"How are you?"

"As you know."

"Yes, I know. This is the result of your actions."

Saying this, Gill also continued on his way, despite Ella's request for him to stay. Ella watched him go and carried on walking. A few steps later, he ran into Bond, his third friend.

"How are things now?"

"As they were."

"It's likely due to sins …"

With that, Bond moved ahead, leaving Ella to continue his solitary journey home.

Listening to the final words of Bond, Ella felt a sense of despair. He lowered himself to the ground, his mind swirling with contemplation. He pondered deeply, questioning the righteousness of his actions. He defiantly asserted that he bore no guilt, attributing his suffering to the injustices ingrained in society. Confusion inundated his thoughts as he grappled with conflicting perspectives; while he saw himself as blameless, his companions painted him as a transgressor. This dissonance left him feeling betrayed by the world's unfairness, igniting a profound sense of anxiety within him.

Ella reached his home and found Leo and Luca in distress, their bodies frail like wooden stems. Despite his efforts to comfort them, they remained restless, yearning to see their mother and younger brothers. Ella, with a heavy heart, explained to them that their loved ones had passed away, but they refused to accept this harsh reality, holding onto the belief that their family was simply away, perhaps bringing treats from the market.

As Ella tried to soothe them, they lashed out in anguish, unable to cope with their grief. Feeling helpless, Ella eventually conceded to their delusion, agreeing that their mother and brothers were indeed on their way home with sweets and biscuits. Yet, their sorrow persisted, and the scene was heart-wrenching to witness.

In an attempt to console them, Ella reassured the boys that they were good children, unlike others, and that their mother would return soon with an abundance of treats. Despite his efforts, the weight of their loss hung heavily in the air, casting a shadow over their home.

Despite Ella's best efforts, Leo and Luca persisted in their sorrow, even resorting to rolling on the ground in anguish. Luca even left the room in his distress, while Leo pleaded with his father to call their mother and brothers. Their grief seemed insurmountable, and Ella's attempts to console them proved futile.

As time passed, concerned members of the community approached Ella in the hope of understanding the cause of the boys' distress. However, Ella remained focused on soothing Leo and Luca, unaware of their inquiries. Despite offering toys, biscuits, toffees, and coins, the boys remained inconsolable, their longing to see their lost loved ones unyielding.

Faced with Leo and Luca's unyielding sorrow, members of the community attempted to console Ella by reminding him of the inevitability of death, a universal law decreed by a higher power. They urged him to find solace in the understanding that his wife and children had simply fulfilled their destined journey in this world, just as everyone eventually did.

The members of the community, explaining this harsh reality before Leo and Luca, served as a reminder that Ella's grief was not unique but rather a shared experience felt by all who walked this earth. They encouraged him to focus on honouring the memory of his departed loved ones through the performance of social and religious rituals, reminding him that his situation was not isolated but part of the collective human experience.

In this way, the community sought to offer Ella comfort by contextualizing his loss within the broader framework of life's inevitable cycles, emphasizing the importance of acceptance and remembrance in the face of adversity.

Despite the promises of assistance and support from the community, Ella remained unconvinced. His memories were clouded by the injustices he had suffered in the past, particularly the illegal occupation of his land and the numerous tragedies he had endured as a result.

Even as others extended their hands in aid, Ella's trust had been eroded by the actions of those who had wronged him before. He could not easily overlook the past grievances and accept the help offered, wary of the intentions behind the promises made.

In his heart, Ella harboured a sense of distrust and resentment, making it difficult for him to embrace the goodwill of others, especially those who had previously caused him harm. Despite the community's gestures of support, Ella remained guarded, unable to forget the injustices of the past.

Once they realized Ella was oblivious to their thoughts, they retreated one by one to the Community Hall, where they dissected Ella's tragedy from various angles. Some attributed his suffering to his supposed wickedness, delving into discussions about his past life. Suggestions flew, painting Ella as a butcher or even likening him to Judas, the infamous betrayer.

In the eyes of the villagers, Ella was branded as the greatest sinner, condemned to a future fraught with sorrow. As they exchanged tales of misfortune from neighbouring villages, it became apparent that Ella's plight was not unique, fuelling their belief in the inevitability of his suffering.

In this moment of communal speculation, it seemed as though the villagers had unravelled the mysteries of Ella's life, weaving together narratives of sin and retribution to explain his tragic circumstances.

Meanwhile, Ella remained within the confines of his home, tending to Leo and Luca amidst the overwhelming weight of his grief. At times, he faltered, his strength waning as if his very breath had ceased. With the villagers gone, he was left alone with his thoughts, his physical needs overshadowed by the turmoil within his soul.

In this state of spiritual turmoil, Ella transcended the mundane aspects of existence. Hunger, thirst, and even sorrow no longer touched him. He appeared as a mere shell, devoid of life's usual desires and emotions. His once vibrant home now lay in disarray, a reflection of the chaos within his being.

Outside, two faithful dogs lingered, their silence speaking volumes of the sorrow that permeated Ella's abode. Tears streamed from their eyes, a silent testament to the tragedy that had befallen their master. Yet, Ella remained oblivious to their presence, consumed by his internal struggle.

As the villagers pondered the mystery behind the dogs' unusual silence, the depth of Ella's suffering became palpable, even in the absence of words.

In the backyard of Ella's home, small trees stood witness to the passage of time, sheltering numerous birds that had made their home there for years. But now, even they seemed restless, their once cheerful chirping replaced by subdued cries. Their weakened voices struggled to carry their sorrow, their eyes mirroring the red hues of dawn.

It was as if the birds had convened a solemn gathering, offering their tribute to Emily, Levi, and Luke. Their mournful melodies echoed through the air, a lament for those who had departed this world of hardship.

In this atmosphere of grief, with only Ella and his sons present, mysterious voices seemed to emanate from different directions, adding to the sense of sorrow that enveloped the scene.

> *O Time! O Immortal Time!*
> *Indeed, you are supreme!*
> *Yes, your art is supreme!*
> *Yes, your seat is supreme!*
>
> *You've seen people weeping,*
> *Laughing, singing, and dancing –*
> *Water to snow – snow to water –*
> *Day to night – night to day.*
>
> *You've seen winter and spring –*
> *Joy and sorrow, life and death –*
> *Water in a boat – a boat in the water –*
> *The moonlight and the sunlight.*
>
> *You watch righteous men and sinners,*
> *Also, the earth and the heaven.*
> *You've seen Judas, Christ, and Christianity;*
> *Your site is like a beam of silk.*
>
> *You have seen Rama and Buddha –*
> *The immortal Moses' seat;*
> *Since ever each prophet;*
> *And they come, never to meet.*

Many passed before eyes;
Lord Gandhi and others died.
You know all – Truth never dies.
The whole world! Peace! Peace! Peace!

It was perhaps one of the elegiac songs sung by Nature. It reminded that every man has to leave this world one day. This song was coming from unknown directions.

Amidst several tragedies, Ella found himself in a quandary. While he grappled with his ocean of sorrows, the villagers remained steadfast in their determination to revel in the annual music show without pause. They seemed oblivious to Ella's plight, unmoved by his need for support in fulfilling the religious rituals and death rites for Emily, Levi, and Luke. Despite the counsel of a few elders advocating for a postponement of the festivities out of respect for Ella's grief, the majority clung staunchly to the belief that tradition must prevail at all costs.

Quoting the verses of the Holy Bible they said to the villagers, *"If there be among you a poor man of one of thy brethren, within any of thy gates in thy land which the LORD thy God giveth thee, thou shalt not harden thine heart, nor shut thine hand from thy poor brother; But thou shalt open thine hand wide unto him, and shalt surely lend him sufficient for his need, in that he wanteth."*

Regardless of Ella's circumstances, the villagers proceeded with the annual music show, revelling in it with unabated joy, seemingly indifferent to Ella's recurring tragedies. The event was marked by extravagant displays of wealth and grandeur, with the majority of villagers enthusiastically partaking in the festivities. Film songs filled the air, delighting the crowd, while comedies entertained and lifted spirits.

Some of the villagers weren't keen on the film songs, calling them obscene. They preferred the folk songs for their lyrical and captivating nature. Consequently, they felt like leaving their seats right from the start of the show. However, after being persuaded by influential individuals to stay and appreciate the stage performance, they remained for a few hours. Yet, shortly after midnight, they departed from the tent and headed towards their homes along the paths.

Meanwhile, an elderly man, aged over a hundred, unexpectedly appeared and positioned himself on the right side of the stage. He questioned, "Is this truly a relief show or merely an extravagant display? Is it a necessary spectacle, particularly when Ella is enduring such hardship?" He denounced it as a contrived exhibition of a superficially civilised society, akin to adding salt to Ella's wounds. His departure followed, yet not a hint of shame graced the faces of the audience who continued to revel in the event. It was akin to rubbing salt into Ella's wounds, leaving him no recourse but to endure and face the afflictions and miseries of his life.

Humanism

Thus, a month went by, but Ella remained unable to return to his normal life. He frequently found himself in dire circumstances, struggling to provide for his children by cultivating crops and foraging for edible plants, which were often scavenged by the destitute as sustenance. He resorted to cooking the roots of winter vegetation found in the local pond. The toll of numerous tragedies and scarce sustenance left him emaciated, resembling more a spectre of bones than a living being with flesh and skin. His protruding bones and sunken eyes spoke of his deprivation, rendering him almost skeletal. Lacking warm clothing to shield himself and his children from the biting cold of winter, they slept on thick straw mats. Once his children were asleep, he would carefully lay another mat over them, before covering himself with yet another to stave off the chill.

In those days, there were numerous cases of exploitation and atrocities against the poor throughout the state. As a result, the Christian missionaries were very active in assisting them. They provided food, clothing, and housing. There was widespread discussion about the role of the missionaries, with some people accusing them of enticing the poor to convert under the guise of humanitarian service. Occasionally, such incidents did occur, but at other times, the missionaries were praised by the local community for their support. There were hundreds of charitable missionaries offering these kinds of services.

Some Hindu religious organisations opposed the missionaries' work in the country. They claimed that hundreds of thousands of Hindus had been converted through various forms of temptation, particularly targeting the most backward areas where people struggled to meet even their basic needs, such as kerosene, electricity, biscuits, and matches. These facilities were a mystery to many. These communities lived in the most remote parts of the country, with no access to education. The government had made efforts to improve their status, but these efforts were only on paper, and no tangible welfare work was evident. People believed that corruption had swallowed the government's welfare schemes. No government welfare work was visible on the ground. Some people had lost faith in the law and the government, expecting no good from either. This disillusionment led some to turn to terrorism, challenging the government and its systems.

However, the missionaries provided their services free of charge and rejected all the accusations made against them. They asserted that humanitarian service was their creed and that they were carrying out their duties with integrity. They challenged anyone to prove that they had enticed individuals to convert from Hinduism to Christianity, insisting that those who chose to convert did so of their own volition, driven by their innermost convictions.

Some Hindu organisations were continuously organising "Home Return" programmes. These programmes aimed to bring back those who had converted from Hinduism to other faiths. However, despite their persistent efforts, only a few families occasionally returned to their former faith. This initiative faced significant criticism from various groups. Clashes between members of the two communities were occurring, and violence was widespread. Numerous new cases of this nature emerged, attracting media attention. The issue gained national prominence, and international news agencies also took it seriously. Correspondents visited remote areas to understand the situation on the ground. They travelled to the most underdeveloped parts of the country, meeting hundreds of families who had converted from Hinduism to Christianity and other faiths.

Subsequently, an interview was released and broadcast by the electronic media:

"Why did you convert from Hinduism to Christianity?"

"All faiths are equal and paths to God. I have neither renounced any religion nor adopted a new one, but rather, I have escaped the hellish conditions caused by exploitation, suppression, injustice, and atrocity. No community came to my aid."

"What is the reason for this?"

"I never felt that I was a human being. The ruling class despised us, treating us as if we were untouchables. They could touch animals but not us – animals were touchable, but we were untouchable to them. They considered us polluting, unlike animals. One can imagine how we could live in such a hellish situation."

"Who do you hold responsible for your sufferings?"

"Especially the ruling class society!"

"How can you accuse this society of being responsible for your suffering?"

"They have corrupted Hinduism. They keep separate utensils for us, believing that if we touch water, it becomes polluted."

"What is your opinion of Hinduism?"

"Hinduism is undoubtedly a very good religion. It is both scientific and spiritual, but the ruling class has utterly degraded it. They exploit religion for their benefit, presenting themselves as agents of God. As a result, we are forced to suffer. Hinduism itself has no wrongs against us; it is the ruling class that has committed every kind of injustice against us."

"Do you welcome the "Home Return" programmes?"

"Never!"

"Why not?"

"We have not forgotten their exploitation, suppression, injustice, and atrocities over the last five thousand years. They have wronged us more than any other group in any society in the world. They worship animals but hate human beings. They have done immense harm to humanity and society."

Some of them boldly stated that a single member of the ruling class society was more dangerous than thousands of members of any other society in the world.

The majority of the lower-class population in the hill and forest areas had converted, and rarely did any of them claim it was due to the temptation of the Christian missionaries. The missionaries had indeed opened new schools in remote areas, and through the usual prayers in these schools, conversions occurred almost automatically, as widely observed. Often, people did not even realise they had converted. Some of them condemned Hinduism, which they believed had condemned them to suffer for generations. They held the ruling-class people responsible for the hardships they endured.

Some Christian missionaries were aware of Ella's hardships and wanted to help him in this critical situation. Meanwhile, James, the Director of Missionaries for Welfare, had travelled to Thane. Upon his return to Durban, he learned the details of Ella's tragedies. Without delay, he left Durban and went to Vellore with a team of ten members, bringing along a doctor, clothing, blankets, family rations, medicines, fruits, and other essential items.

The doctor immediately began treating Ella and his children. The team cleaned Ella's filthy hut and bathed him and his children. James provided them with new clothes, and the old straw mat they had been using was burnt by the bank of the Toss River. He also supplied three beds, three cushions, three bed sheets, and six blankets. He assigned two workers to care for them until they regained their health. These workers bathed them daily and provided nutritious food, fruits, and essential minerals and vitamins. James personally visited them every day to check on their mental and physical well-being.

Ella was utterly despondent, having lost all faith in life. He anticipated suffering the same fate as his wife and two young sons. He often raised questions, to which James would respond by quoting verses from the Holy Bible.

"This is real life … The name of sorrows …"

"Blessed is the man who walketh not in the counsel of ungodly, nor standeth in the way of sinners, nor sitteth in the seat of the scornful. But his delight is in the law of Lord; and in his law doth he meditate day and night."

"They ever gain and I ever lose."

"For Lord knoweth the way of the righteous: but the way of the ungodly shall perish."

"Is the Lord just?"

"Absolutely."

"Come back, O Lord, rescue my soul; save me for the sake of your mercy."

"The Lord will administer His judgment in due time."

After about a month had passed, James noticed that Ella and his two sons had returned to their normal lives. With this in mind, he began his service for the second phase. This phase involved providing a brick-built house, a hand-pump for drinking water, training Ella in toy-making for livelihood, education for Leo and Luca, and other essential items – all provided completely free of charge.

Upon learning of this plan, Ella's lost smile reappeared on his face, radiant once again. On that very day, James arranged for bricks, cement, iron rods, and other necessary materials for constructing a new house.

The following morning, Ella, along with some labourers, commenced demolishing his mud-built house and began laying the foundation for the new one. However, when Harris discovered their actions, he arrived at the site accompanied by his bodyguard and ordered them to be assaulted. Consequently, they were subjected to severe beatings. As a result, Ella decided to postpone building the new house for the time being.

Now Ella had no place to call home except the open sky. That night, he endured the cold under a peepal tree near the Community Hall. Leo, Luca, and two members of the Missionaries for Welfare also spent the night with

Ella. However, when James learned of the progress in building a new house for Ella the next morning, he was visibly distressed. Ella recounted to him all that had transpired the previous day.

Aware of the circumstances, James advised Ella to make himself comfortable in Durban, a suburb of Cester, given the seriousness of the situation. Clearly, he had no alternative but to depart from the location where he had been deprived of tranquillity, relaxation, and happiness by a powerful individual. Thus, he prepared himself to relocate there.

On that very day, he departed from Vellore to Durban alongside James, taking up residence in the same household. The following day, he enrolled both of his sons at St Xavier School in Durban. Within a month, a modest brick house was constructed close to the school, where Ella, Leo, and Luca settled in.

After some time, he secured a position as a school gardener. This marked Ella's return to a semblance of normality alongside Leo and Luca, following his dedicated service by James to them. As time elapsed, he felt a newfound enlightenment dawning within his mind and heart. He witnessed a vibrant spring, adorned with countless daffodils singing and dancing with joy, a stark contrast to his past experiences. He sensed a profound transformation within himself, experiencing immense happiness. Just two months later, Ella, without any coercion, expressed his desire to James for himself and his children to convert from Hinduism to Christianity. James relayed this request to the head of the Christian Society with humility and impartiality. Upon learning of this, permission was granted for their conversion, and they were formally converted in a religious ceremony. Their names were changed accordingly, with Ella, Leo, and Luca becoming Jesus Smith, John, and Joy, respectively. They embraced the rituals and customs of Christianity, commencing their prayers at the nearest church. From then on, he was known as Jesus Smith, although people commonly referred to him simply as "Jesus".

At present, Jesus appeared transformed not just outwardly but also spiritually. Residing in a modest brick apartment with his two children, their attire had undergone a change; now opting for trousers and shirts instead of traditional dhotis and kurtas. His children appeared rejuvenated and content, also donning trousers and shirts. They regularly attended prayers at the nearby church, embodying a sense of liberation from the centuries-old oppression, suppression, and exploitation stemming from caste prejudice.

Thus, their once beds of misery and sorrow were now adorned with happiness and delight. Their transformation was so profound that it became difficult to recognize them, considering their previous living conditions in Vellore akin to destitute creatures, contrasted with their true essence as genuine human beings in Durban. Radiant smiles graced their faces, and they took pride in introducing themselves as Jesus Smith, John, and Joy.

Upon learning of Ella's conversion to Christianity, along with Leo and Luca, the people of Vellore were overcome with shame and anger. They lamented that had they supported Ella in his time of need, he wouldn't have felt compelled to convert. Discussions ensued about the various societal evils and their own indifference towards a man facing urgent troubles. Someone among them even invoked the aphorism, *A Man in Need is a Friend Indeed*, acknowledging their failure to uphold this principle in Ella's case.

They conceded that their neglect of Ella's plight, exacerbated by societal pressures, was the primary reason for his conversion. They contrasted their society, steeped in notions of hierarchy, with the Christian community, which demonstrated love, compassion, mercy, sympathy, and a sense of responsibility towards those in distress. With Ella gone, they bemoaned the loss of their dependable servant who had always been ready to serve them on various occasions such as annual shows and weddings. They fretted over who would now fulfil these duties and obey their commands. His departure was seen as a significant loss not just for Vellore but also for their religion.

Blaming James for deceiving them, they felt a deep sense of shame and resolved to prevent further conversions in the future. They feared that if they failed to address this issue, their religion would be in jeopardy, and they themselves might be forced to convert eventually. Their anxiety over these prospects led them to take the matter very seriously.

Upon hearing of Ella's conversion, Harris chuckled and remarked sarcastically that once Ella was merely a servant of the village, but now he went by the name Jesus Smith. He likened Ella's appearance to that of a pig, yet now he bore a title akin to a nobleman. Harris cynically pondered who would come to the aid of Jesus in the future.

The villagers grew highly critical of the Christian society, a departure from their typically liberal and tolerant disposition. They treated this matter with utmost seriousness, akin to how certain Hindu organizations addressed issues concerning Christian missionaries. They sought to put forth a resolution aimed at preventing future conversions within their villages. While not all, a significant portion of their society displayed unjust attitudes, neglecting their duty towards those in need. Instead of addressing the root causes prompting conversions to other faiths, they harboured a desire for retribution following Ella's conversion.

Recognizing the potential ramifications if this trend persisted, they convened a meeting in the Community Hall. Representatives from various castes, particularly Hindus, participated in the discussion. Together, they proposed measures against the Christian society in response to their grievances.

The motion was carried with full agreement. Consequently, the Secretary of the society stepped onto the stage to express gratitude.

He remarked, "I extend my heartfelt thanks for endorsing the resolution, marking a significant milestone in Vellore's history."

He reiterated, "I hereby adjourn the meeting." As attendees prepared to leave, an elderly gentleman, seated outside the Community Hall, called out to them, requesting a brief pause.

Thus, they halted momentarily.

He began by asserting that they bore responsibility as stewards of religion and society. He urged them to introspect rather than targeting the Christian community with resolutions. He posed a series of questions: Do you assist those in need? If not, how do you prevent them from converting? Why? How? Do you have valid answers to these inquiries? Have you considered the prevalent societal ills? Why not? Do you overlook the fact that millions of Hindus convert to Christianity annually in our country? Have you contemplated the reasons behind their conversions? He raised numerous societal concerns. He advocated for self-reflection, urging them to earnestly consider their actions. He pointed out that despite the passage of several bills by parliament aimed at uplifting the weaker sections of society, little tangible progress had been made. He queried whether they condoned such inequities at both the social and grassroots levels.

They were taken aback when the old man approached them and chastised them for overlooking significant issues. Consequently, they became solemn and earnest.

Despite lacking a response, they remained silent. Once more, he pressed, "Gentlemen! Can any of you provide a justified response? Please, anyone, tell me. Why? Why not?"

Yet, their silence persisted, as they found themselves unable to articulate a suitable reply.

He persisted, asserting his understanding and their lack of a response. He likened them to hollow oaks, devoid of substance. He implored them to listen attentively if they were unaware. Drawing from his extensive life experience of 125 years, he highlighted the inadequacy of their society in assisting those in need. He emphasized that had they aided Ella in her dire situation, he wouldn't have converted to Christianity. However, he stressed that this wasn't enough. He challenged them to acknowledge the pervasive evil of untouchability within their society, where even Hindus were not treated as such. He questioned who truly constituted Hindus, including the untouchables, whom they didn't regard as equals. He insisted that without addressing their welfare, continuous conversions would persist. He urged them to recognize the untouchables as their own and to strive for their social, economic, and educational upliftment. He warned that without their welfare, achieving integration would remain a mere illusion. Therefore, he urged the abolition of such evils, suggesting that even God couldn't halt conversions without societal reform. His insightful ideas had the power to resonate deeply with their hearts and minds.

Upon hearing his compelling arguments, they reconvened for another meeting. In a significant turn of events, the Secretary himself resigned from his position. Consequently, they nominated another individual to take up the role of Secretary.

Following his nomination, he rose to address the assembly. Expressing gratitude, he thanked them profusely for entrusting him with the responsibility as a leader in the village and society. He acknowledged the significance of this role and accepted the challenge wholeheartedly. He pledged to dedicate himself to the betterment of their society, village, and religious community, promising to work tirelessly towards their welfare.

The villagers unanimously passed the reformation bill during the meeting. Additionally, they made the decision to conduct the death rites and a death feast for Emily, Levi, and Luke. Despite several months passing, Jesus had not arranged for their proper ceremonies and had relocated to Durban. Consequently, the villagers collected donations to facilitate these rites and the subsequent feast.

After the meeting, they proceeded to the location where Levi and Luke had been previously buried by Jesus. Carefully, they exhumed their decomposed bodies and reinterred them in the designated burial ground, following the Hindu tradition which dictates burial for minors rather than cremation. Once the solemn task was completed, they returned to their respective homes.

The following day, they extended invitations to Brahmins to conduct

Emily's death rituals, marking the second day of observance. On the tenth day, following tradition, they summoned eleven Brahmins to perform the rituals of that day. On this significant occasion, they presented the Brahmins with various items, including a bed, a chair, two cushions, bed linens, a sari, a cow, one quintal of basmati rice, 11 kilograms of pigeon-pea pulses, curd, milk, and sugar. These offerings were intended to be sent to Emily's spirit in heaven as part of the ritual observance.

On the tenth day, as part of the rituals, a group of villagers journeyed to Banaras with Emily's ashes to be dispersed in the sacred Ganges River. There, they encountered a Hindu priest adorned with red sandalwood paste on his forehead, a traditional marker of his priestly status, distinguishable by his red attire. The priest accepted a donation of five thousand rupees from the villagers and conducted the immersion ceremony. Subsequently, Emily's ashes were reverently dispersed into the holy waters of the Ganges.

On the thirteenth day since the commencement of Emily's death rituals, they arranged for one hundred and one Brahmins to conduct the death-feast rituals for Emily, Levi, and Luke. During the festivities, the Brahmins performed the death-feast rituals, finding spiritual satisfaction rather than merely physical nourishment. The event surpassed all previous records for such celebrations of its kind, marking a significant and memorable occasion.

On that same day, they had extended an invitation to Harris, but unfortunately, he couldn't participate as he was occupied with parliamentary sessions in New Delhi. Two days after the death feast, they convened another meeting to evaluate their management of the event. The majority of attendees expressed satisfaction, recognizing their successful execution of the daunting task.

The Treasurer of the society informed them that the actual expenditure for the celebration was lower than the collected amount. This news brought joy to the villagers, reassuring them that everything had been managed efficiently, and they looked forward to similar successes in the future. The Treasurer and others expressed their happiness with loud applause. Subsequently, the Secretary was called upon to deliver the vote of thanks.

As he delivered the vote of thanks to society, he reminded everyone of Emily's faithful service as their maid from her honeymoon until the day she fell ill and departed from this world. He emphasized that it was because of her dedicated service that, when Ella performed the final rites and lit the funeral pyre, the priest recited the sacred hymns to guide her soul to heaven, as per their beliefs.

He continued, expressing that the secretary held a deep affection for Emily's children. It was evident in his regular provision of food for them, ensuring their well-being. He regarded them as his cherished ones. Furthermore, he didn't hesitate to acknowledge Emily's attachment to his family. She was the pulse of their household, tirelessly serving them and placing their needs above all else. Her dedication knew no bounds; she never refused any task and wholeheartedly followed their orders. He lamented that if she were still with them, Ella wouldn't have made the grave error of conversion, a mistake that would haunt him for a lifetime. The mere mention of his name, Jesus Smith, filled him, the Secretary, with shame, a reminder of the profound mistake Ella ad made by assuming the name "Jesus", tarnishing its sanctity.

People expressed immense satisfaction and joy with his sentiments. They hailed him as a great man and a genuine advocate for the downtrodden and impoverished. They viewed him as their leader, guiding light, and decisive force. This acknowledgement underscored the profound impact of his ideas and actions on the community.

In the ensuing silence, the Secretary rose to his feet and announced, "The meeting stands adjourned until further notice."

With those final words, the meeting concluded, and attendees dispersed to their respective homes. As they departed, they engaged in discussions, reflecting on the matter from various angles and recognizing their collective responsibility for fostering such remarkable unity within the society.

The Walk for Justice

Some months had passed. Jesus had not forgotten Harris's injustice. He found new zeal and courage. Determined to obtain justice at any cost, he sought advice from his neighbours, who encouraged him to pursue it. Consequently, he decided to go to the court of the Circle Officer in Chester to seek justice for the wrong done by Harris, which had resulted in the loss of his paternal land some months before.

It was Monday – a day with a scorching sun in the summer season. Jesus went to the Circle Officer in Chester and submitted his petition against the injustice done to him by Harris.

The officer took his petition in hand, looked at him sternly, and said, "Go away and return on Wednesday with all the supporting documents."

After submitting the documents and completing the necessary official formalities, both parties were summoned to appear in court for the trial. The trial date was also set.

The court session started in the morning. The following Wednesday, Jesus arrived at the court at 7 a.m., carrying a wallet full of supporting documents in his right hand. He sat on the adjacent veranda, waiting for his summons from the court. While sitting there, he noticed Harris sitting directly before the officer in the court, and they were having tea together. This sight made him doubt that Harris would undoubtedly have the advantage in the case due to his close relationship with the officer. Feeling very depressed, he began to pace back and forth on the veranda.

Meanwhile, he was summoned to court. As he entered, he submitted all his supporting documents to the officer's assistant and stood on the left side. He felt very afraid because of Harris's bodyguard, who was standing inside the court with a long, conical moustache, a long black beard, and a rifle in his right hand. The clerk handed the documents to the officer, who spent several minutes reading them, though he seemed to turn the pages more than read them. There was no motion and no comment.

Later on, the officer asked Jesus, "Had Lila, who was your father, ever sold the said land?"

"No, Sir! No, Sir! Never! My father never sold any land in his entire life!" Jesus replied.

The officer said again, "But when I examined the sale deed and all the documents related to the case, I found that your father had sold the said land during his lifetime."

Meanwhile, Harris was smiling smugly.

Upon hearing this, he said, "That's correct. Absolutely right! I bought it from his father."

The defence counsel stood up and addressed the honourable judge, stating that Harris, his client, had purchased the land for fifty thousand rupees from Jesus's elderly father about eleven years before. He asserted that his client was a very honest and honourable politician and a well-known Member of Parliament from the New Socialist Party. He emphasised Harris's kindness and dedication to serving the poor and suffering. The counsel argued that Harris could never commit such an offence against a poor man like Jesus and pointed out Harris's virtue by noting that he had allowed Jesus to use the land for the last eleven years so he could earn a living.

He continued, affirming that Harris was a well-respected political figure with an impeccable reputation. He argued that Harris had become a victim of the malicious intentions of Jesus and his Christian community, unjustly compelled to face legal proceedings in the court. He portrayed Jesus as a morally dubious individual who had converted from Hinduism to Christianity solely for economic gain and a better life. According to the counsel, Jesus's character was highly questionable, as he attempted to unlawfully claim land that had been sold by his father eleven years prior. Therefore, the counsel implored the judge for justice and urged the dismissal of the case, proposing that Jesus be ordered to pay twenty thousand rupees in compensation and an additional two thousand rupees to cover Harris's expenses.

In the meantime, Jesus stood in the court like an immovable object, rooted in the room. He remained silent, desperately wanting to speak but unable to utter a single word.

Meanwhile, the officer interjected, "Jesus, do you wish to add anything further?"

"Y...e...s... sir... n...o... sir," Jesus stuttered.

The officer retorted, "What kind of response is that? Either speak clearly or leave this courtroom."

Jesus regained his composure and respectfully stated that all his documents had been submitted to the court. He affirmed that he had been diligently paying the land revenue at the officer's office for years, including the current year. He adamantly asserted that neither his father nor his ancestors had ever sold any land, and thus, the purported sale deed was undoubtedly fraudulent.

Harris couldn't contain himself and began hurling abusive words, demanding that Jesus remain silent and leave immediately. His menacing bodyguard even brandished the rifle, instilling fear in Jesus, who promptly left the courtroom.

Outside, Jesus sat in the connected veranda, while Harris and the officer indulged in sweets and oranges inside. Occasionally, they carelessly tossed orange peels out of the window, some landing on Jesus without his notice as he was consumed by the court proceedings.

However, when Harris's bodyguard threw a stone at him, Jesus snapped out of his reverie and departed the area.

The relentless insults, injustices, and exploitation he endured were beyond comprehension, turning his life into a living nightmare.

And so, half an hour passed in this distressing manner.

Meanwhile, the officer pondered aloud, "What should be done?"

Harris remained silent, instead retrieving a sealed envelope from the pocket of his Gandhi coat, symbolizing his adherence to Mahatma Gandhi's principles. The officer accepted the envelope and placed it on his diary, which rested on the table.

Unintentionally, the diary slipped off the table and onto the floor. However, the officer quickly retrieved the sealed envelope and returned it to his pocket.

After some time, Harris exited the court and settled into his car. Soon, the vehicle began its journey along the roads leading to Cester City.

Observing Harris's departure, Jesus approached the court clerk and inquired, "What happened?"

The clerk dismissed him curtly, saying, "Nothing! Go away. Return here next Saturday."

With no further recourse, Jesus returned home.

He arrived home burdened with uncertainty and a heavy heart. Contemplating his next steps, he held onto the hope of achieving justice, unaware of the harsh realities that surrounded him. Expecting the officer to rule in his favour and restore his property, he remained deeply absorbed in thought. Turning to prayer, he sought solace and divine intervention.

"My heart is deeply troubled, and the fear of death grips me," he uttered. "Save me, O God!"

The following day, the Circle Officer arrived at the location in Vellore for an inquiry. Harris, Jesus, and several other individuals were also present at the site. The officer inspected the disputed land, moving around it numerous times. Observing his presence, additional villagers also gathered at the spot.

The Circle Officer proceeded to question the people present regarding Ella and his land. Inquiring whether they were acquainted with Jesus, the responses were consistently negative, with individuals claiming not to know him.

Persisting with his line of questioning, the officer reiterated that Jesus was the new name for Ella, who stood before them.

Upon learning of his new name, they affirmed their acquaintance with Jesus, acknowledging him as a former resident of their village and speaking highly of his character.

They described him as a good and obedient man, always willing to assist whenever needed, and regarded him as a gentleman.

When asked about the ownership of the land – whether it belonged to Jesus or Harris – they evaded a direct response, claiming ignorance on the matter.

The officer, puzzled by their reluctance, inquired whether they resided in Vellore or not.

However, they shamelessly admitted to living in the village but asserted that they were preoccupied with their responsibilities, thus implying their detachment from local affairs.

Despite their initial reluctance, the officer persisted in his inquiries, probing whether they had ever visited Jesus's home during his time in the village.

Responding affirmatively, they recounted their visits to his home, highlighting Jesus's unwavering dedication to serving their needs. They expressed admiration for his willingness to assist them promptly, regardless of the hour or weather conditions. They regarded him as a true and honest individual, lamenting that their village had suffered in his absence since his departure for Vellore. Reflecting on his departure, they expressed sorrow and nostalgia, considering Jesus to have been an esteemed figure in their community. They concluded that they had never encountered anyone as virtuous as him.

When questioned about the location of Jesus's house, the villagers, fearing Harris's wrath, refused to divulge any information. Despite there being over one hundred people present, none dared to disclose where Jesus resided or where he cultivated vegetables. Within a matter of minutes, they dispersed one by one, illustrating their reluctance to assist Jesus, particularly in adverse circumstances. This reluctance to aid Jesus on rainy days was widely acknowledged.

Left alone, Jesus himself provided detailed information about the location of his modest mud-built house and the field where he had cultivated vegetables for years. He emphasized that this was his ancestral land, passed down through generations, and expressed his deep anguish at its loss. To him, this land was not just property but an integral part of his existence, and its loss weighed heavily on his heart.

As Jesus poured out his heartfelt anguish, the officer listened attentively, nodding in apparent understanding. However, unbeknownst to Jesus, an internal conflict raged within the officer. He had already accepted a substantial bribe enclosed in the envelope to ensure a ruling in Harris's favour. His presence at the inquiry was merely a formality, as he felt powerless to deliver a judgment against Harris in a system where "might is right" prevailed.

The pervasive culture of corruption had paralyzed the entire government system, leaving minimal hope for Jesus's victory in the case. Corruption was rampant at all levels of employment, with only a handful of individuals remaining untainted by its influence.

Despite being fully aware of the pervasive corruption and the daunting odds stacked against him, Jesus remained steadfast in his resolve to pursue justice. His unwavering commitment seemed to stem from a spiritual fortitude that emboldened him. Though he might not have possessed the physical charm of Harris, his inner strength and integrity far surpassed his adversary's.

To Jesus, accepting exploitation and oppression was tantamount to endorsing them. He firmly believed that those who failed to resist such injustices were complicit in perpetuating them. Advocating for righteous struggle, he urged everyone he encountered to join the fight for justice.

Furthermore, Jesus emphasized the importance of self-reliance, asserting that divine assistance was bestowed upon those who took action to help themselves. With unwavering honesty and fearlessness, Jesus candidly shared his ideals with the officer, determined to stand up for what he believed was right.

Intent on maximizing the bribe from Harris, the officer instructed Jesus to return home and meet him in court the following Saturday. With that, he settled into his car, ready to depart from the scene.

As the officer was about to leave, a stranger approached him, inquiring about the purpose of his presence at the location.

The stranger was curious about the reason for the large crowd gathered there.

In response, the officer addressed the stranger, saying, "My friend, are you aware of the land issue?"

The stranger responded firmly in the affirmative, stating that he was well acquainted with the past, present, and future of the land. Intrigued by this assertion, the officer urged the stranger to elaborate on his knowledge of the land. Without hesitation, the stranger began to recount what he knew.

The stranger asserted his profound knowledge of the land, affirming that it rightfully belonged to Ella, with his ancestors having inhabited and cultivated it for centuries. However, tragedy befell Ella, the village, the society, and humanity at large when Harris, wielding his influence, unlawfully seized and forcibly occupied the land, driving Ella from his home. The stranger emphasized the proximity of divine justice, assuring that it would inevitably prevail in due course. He urged everyone to acknowledge this divine truth, as it could not be disregarded or overlooked.

After delivering his message, the old man mysteriously vanished, leaving the officer perplexed for a moment.

The officer found himself contemplating the matter earnestly, astonished by the strange occurrence of the stranger's sudden disappearance. Such inexplicable events were unprecedented in his experience.

Caught between his inability to deliver a judgment against Harris and the revelation of the facts of the case, the officer found himself in a dilemma. He struggled to find the right course of action, rendered speechless and deep in thought for several minutes.

Eventually, he broke the silence, uttering, "Oh my God! Please forgive me! I will never …" His sentence remained unfinished as he stood there, lost in contemplation.

Finally, after some time, he instructed Jesus to appear in court on the day of the hearing and then departed from the scene, his mind heavy with the weight of his decision.

I Wanted to Weep

Not all, but most of the officers act in favour of influential individuals, taking government laws into their own hands and disregarding the facts. This is very common in most offices. Some honest officers have suffered in every aspect of their lives because the influential individuals have harassed them. In this context, the Circle Officer was also in favour of Harris, ignoring all the facts.

Thus, the Circle Officer accompanied Harris to a five-star hotel. The hotel was marvellous, a multi-storeyed building and the most renowned hotel in Cester, situated in a crowded market. Its name and quality were indistinguishable, and it resembled the palace or castle of a great king or emperor. The front wall of the hotel was designed in the style of Khajuraho architecture, adorned with several paintings of erotic scenes. The front wall of the hotel featured some lines from William Butler Yeats's "Sailing to Byzantium":

> *Once out of nature, I shall never take*
> *My bodily form any natural thing,*
> *But such a form as Grecian goldsmiths make*
> *Of hammered gold and gold enamelling*
> *To keep drowsy Emperor awake;*
> *Or set upon a golden bough to sing*
> *To lords and ladies of Byzantium*
> *Of what is past, or passing, or to come.*

He read the inscribed lines very carefully. His cheeks began to glow, and a deep smile appeared on his face. He forgot about the issue of the spot inquiry, now entranced by the charms and beauty of the hotel.

The hotel featured a large lawn, an auditorium, a park with blooming flowers, and an artificial fountain. Its marbled and decorated walls and floors glittered like glass. The exterior walls were golden-coloured, and each room was air-conditioned. Every room had a colour television with a music player. The sofa sets and beds in each room were made of sandalwood and covered with luxurious cushions and velvet fabrics. There was an en-suite bathroom in every room.

The management of the hotel also provided beautiful call girls according to the demand of customers. The hire rate of a single room was fifty thousand rupees for twenty-four hours, with an extra payment for a call girl.

It was Friday. Two rooms – 101 and 102 – were allocated to Harris and the Circle Officer, respectively. They arrived at 7 p.m., sat in the dining room, and discussed the land issue in detail for hours. During this time, they appeared like hunters – not of animals or birds, but of sex – with guilty smiles on their faces.

After their discussion, Harris looked very pleased. At one point, he remarked with satisfaction that the communist leaders had indeed ignited a fire in the country. They used to chant about equality … equality … But what relevance did it have in society? They didn't understand. It was impossible in Indian society. Harris, with his extensive experience, observed that the poor advocated for the redistribution of the rich's property. They wanted to implement communism, but Harris and his supporters opposed it. He said it was very harmful to them and the country. He believed that the officer understood all this. According to Harris, even Jesus would have gone mad listening to such ideology, failing to grasp the strong roots of Indian aristocracy. He felt Jesus's victory was as easy as buying a pen or paper. But the fact was that, regardless of the law, victory would always be in favour of Harris. History was its witness. He said Jesus had gone mad and didn't understand all this, but in time, Jesus would come to witness it.

He continued to express his views, questioning why Jesus would live if he were poor. He asserted that the poor were indeed the greatest enemies of the rich, constantly thinking about redistributing the wealth of the rich. If they were poor, he argued, they should die. Their ideas revealed their true intentions.

The officer supported him and said to let it go. He assured Harris that he was ready to do anything for him and felt as if he himself might die soon upon hearing his decision.

After their dinner, they entered their allotted rooms, where they were welcomed by night queens who looked like fairies. All this was a common practice for Harris and the officer.

Upon entering, they turned to the queens, embraced them, kissed them, and lay on the luxurious beds. Soon they switched on their colour televisions, began to watch blue films, and enjoyed the company of those fairies the whole night.

The next morning, when they rose, they looked like lost men – lost in the experiences of the night. Both were in a serious mood.

In the meantime, Harris said to the officer that she was indeed a fairy – she had made the previous night unforgettable. Therefore, fifty thousand rupees for each one was not spent in vain.

The officer also concurred and expressed his feelings. He said that the previous night was equally unforgettable for him. The night had been heaven on earth.

Undoubtedly, they were the true fate determiners of the world, which was once regarded as a holy place but is now a place where all are pale and ailing. They felt proud of such deeds, and not a single ray of shame was seen on their faces. They enjoyed the night and shared their experiences in the morning. After having breakfast, they departed to go to court.

It was Saturday. The trial was set to begin in the court of the Circle Officer in Cester. Jesus arrived there at seven o'clock in the morning and sat outside the court, waiting impatiently for his call. He spent four hours like this, but he didn't catch even a glimpse of Harris or the Circle Officer.

After a few more minutes, he noticed that the counsel for the defence was sitting in the darkest part of the court, chewing betel. The counsel's smile was sweet, suggesting he had gained something.

Seeing him, Jesus fell into a dilemma and began to mutter, "What's the matter?" He also wondered if the hearing might be postponed to a later date.

In the meantime, two cars arrived and stopped – one belonging to Harris and the other to the officer. Upon seeing this, the peon came to receive the officer. Meanwhile, Jesus's heart was palpitating rapidly. When the officer emerged from the car, his first glance fell on Jesus, and he looked at him like a hound before moving towards the court. Harris followed him, and both took their seats in the courtroom. The officer sat down and told Harris to sit as well. Once seated, he demanded the file for Jesus's case. Within a minute, the clerk placed the file before him, and he ordered the peon to call Jesus.

When Jesus entered the court, he saw the officer writing something on the file. He stood still in front of the officer, noticing that Harris and his counsel seemed very happy while the officer was in a serious mood. Harris was chewing saffron, and the officer was writing quickly and continuously, as if preparing a "research paper." For twenty-five minutes, the officer didn't speak a single word to anyone. Finally, he uttered just one sentence: "The case … is dismissed."

The officer himself felt responsible for his actions, whether they were right or wrong. Therefore, he didn't stay for long, and after expressing his legal "discovery," he left the court. As he exited, Harris also left with his bodyguard, heading towards the path that led to Harris Palace.

After they had gone, Jesus approached the clerk and asked, "What …? Has the case been dismissed?"

The clerk replied, "Go outside and you can read it on the notice board in an hour."

However, Jesus was very anxious to know the judgement delivered by the Circle Officer. His forehead was damp with sweat. Unable to wait, he approached the clerk again after just five minutes and pleaded, "Sir, please, tell me what 'dismiss' means?"

The clerk, becoming furious, retorted, "Oh, foolish man! What dismiss-fish-miss? Go away at once, and don't come to me again."

Feeling dejected, Jesus left the court soon after.

To pass the time, Jesus began to move hither and thither on the veranda of the court like a madman. After an hour, the peon came and hung the decision on the notice board. Seeing this, Jesus went over and asked a stranger to read the notice for him because he was too nervous and quite unable to read it himself.

The stranger began to read: "After legal consideration of the case, the court comes to the conclusion that the father of Jesus had sold this land for fifty thousand rupees. The court, therefore, dismisses the case and orders Jesus to pay twenty thousand rupees as compensation for using the said land for the last eleven years, and two thousand rupees as costs to Harris, within fifteen days. If there is a delay, he will have to pay the said amount with twelve per cent interest. The decision comes into force with my signature and the seal of this court."

Hearing this, Jesus fainted and fell to the ground. People gathered around him, splashing water on his face. After ten minutes, he regained consciousness and sat on the ground. Curious onlookers came and went, trying to find out why he had fainted, but he did not utter a single word and remained in the same state for two hours.

Over the next two hours, everyone gradually left the court, leaving Jesus alone. Around 2 p.m., the watchman came to close the main gate of the court and found Jesus lying there, his clothes covered in dust and sweat.

Seeing this, the watchman grabbed Jesus by both feet and began to drag him out. Finally, he pulled him out of the gate into the scorching sun and onto the hot, dusty ground, showing no mercy.

Meanwhile, a passer-by was walking by, chanting a poem by Gauri Deshpande entitled "I Wanted to Weep":

> *I wanted to weep for you*
> *And me*
> *But I had already spent*
> *All tears in useless mournings.*
> *So now I watch arideyed*
> *As many fingers open slowly*
> *And let you go.*

Jesus also listened to the poem chanted by the passer-by, and he began to reflect on himself and the world. The lines pierced his heart and mind. He said, "Alas," and became serious. After a moment, some words escaped his lips: "Have mercy upon me, O God!"

After a few more moments, Jesus regained his strength and stood up. However, he found that his pockets were empty, his wallet was gone, and his slippers were missing. A thief had stolen them, proving that misfortunes never come alone.

Despite the hot ground and the scorching sun, Jesus made his way to Durban along paths shaded by trees. Whenever the ground became too hot for his bare legs to bear, he either stood or sat in the shade of the trees. He arrived in Durban at 5 p.m.

There, James had been eagerly awaiting Jesus. When Jesus didn't arrive, James went to his house and found him lying on the wooden bed, looking exhausted like a weary soldier.

Seeing James, Jesus stood up and fetched a chair for him. James asked Jesus to explain the reason for his delay, so Jesus recounted everything that had happened to him in the court of the Circle Officer.

Upon hearing Jesus's story, James said, "Let it go. Forget about it completely. Stay on the right path. God will surely help you. God tests us in various ways. Wait for His decision, and forget about the officer's ruling."

He reiterated that Jesus must remember that God was omnipotent, and in His presence, even the smallest being couldn't be equalled by man. He advised Jesus to patiently await divine justice, which would inevitably come in due time.

A neighbour of Jesus also approached him and offered words of encouragement. He assured Jesus that he was brave and shouldn't worry. He pointed out that Harris's victory was likely the result of bribery – a practice common among politicians and bureaucrats. Therefore, it shouldn't be a cause for despair. He reminded Jesus of John Milton's words, "They also serve who only stand and wait."

Their consolation and inspiring words were like soothing rays of balm to Jesus. He felt revitalized by James and his neighbours' encouragement. Their words filled him with energy.

He prayed, "O Lord, judge me! For I have walked in my integrity. I have trusted in the Lord. Therefore, I shall not stray from the path of righteousness."

Meanwhile, after Harris's victory in the case, a celebration of the love feast took place at the Harris Palace. A large tent was set up in the courtyard, resembling a bride. Rows of cushioned chairs were arranged for the guests, who wandered around admiring the setup. They enjoyed the feast wholeheartedly. Harris had invited his relatives and friends, and guests began to arrive at 5 p.m. However, the Circle Officer had arrived earlier in the morning. He managed the feast and appeared as the head of Harris's family.

Some people speculated that the Circle Officer might be a relative of Harris, as he was seen receiving all incoming guests and ushering them to their seats. On the right side of the tent gate, Harris sat on a majestic chair crafted from sandalwood, resembling a sage. Each guest entered the tent after paying their respects to him.

Upon taking their seats, guests were presented with silver packets adorned with the labels of "Heavenly Sweets," containing modern confections in vogue, along with a piece of vegetable chop. After consuming one or two sweets, they casually discarded the packets onto the ground. As they did so, they were promptly offered bottles of branded wine. They swiftly broke the seals and indulged in the contents, creating an atmosphere of heavenly bliss.

However, such bliss was absent in Jesus's home, where he and his neighbours were plunged into deep distress, and a sense of despair and sadness seemed to envelop all of Durban.

On the other hand, some viewed the situation differently. They saw the feast not as a celebration of justice prevailing over injustice, but rather as a triumph of injustice over justice. It was perceived as the powerful oppressing the poor, the rich exploiting the less fortunate, the capable suppressing the incapable, and humanity's betrayal of its core values. This was deemed a matter of great shame for humanity as a whole.

Critics directed their ire towards Harris, branding his actions as a stain on the sanctity of the earth and humanity. They viewed it as a heinous crime against the principles of humanism, a display of worldly power rather than divine authority. It was likened to a marketplace where Harris traded away his honesty, brotherhood, morality, and humanity for personal gain.

There was a vivid and poignant display of poverty unfolding before the eyes of onlookers. It was a scene that demanded serious contemplation. As the feast concluded, Harris instructed his servants to discard the leftover sweets, packets, and wine bottles outside the tent, into a muddy and dirty brook. Without hesitation, they complied.

The untouchables of Cester awaited their chance eagerly. As the defiled sweets, wine bottles, and packets were tossed aside, they rushed towards them like hungry hunters, seizing the opportunity to consume with both hands. Some even seized the empty wine bottles, hoping to sell them in the market for a few coins to purchase tobacco or opium. Their greatest adversaries were not wealthy individuals, but rather the dogs who shared in the discarded and defiled sweets. These were not their pets, but rather stray dogs scavenging for food alongside them. Sometimes, they fought over the food, with both hungry people and dogs resorting to snatching from each other.

In this chaotic struggle for sustenance amidst the muddy brook, six men were bitten by dogs. The following morning, those who had collected empty wine bottles ventured to the market and sold them. With the coins earned, they experienced a sense of utmost pleasure as they indulged in tobacco, opium, or even gambling.

Instead of seeking medical attention at a hospital, the individuals bitten by dogs took matters into their own hands. They embarked on a journey to visit fourteen wells, a traditional method of treatment to protect themselves from hydrophobia, a prevalent danger in the area. This age-old practice had been passed down for centuries. Eventually, they resumed their daily routines, putting the incident behind them.

Those who had partaken in the discarded sweets expressed great satisfaction, feeling that the feast had been meant for them alone. They teased the unfortunate souls who had missed out on the opportunity to indulge in the thrown and defiled sweets from the brook. Those who had also collected empty wine bottles were even happier, as they had enjoyed both the sweets and the makeshift wine the following morning. They had washed the bottles with water and savoured the liquid joyfully before selling them in the market.

After the feast, the guests departed from the Harris Palace and returned to their respective homes. However, the Circle Officer chose to spend the night in the palace, accompanied by a call girl.

The following morning, he rose late. After going through his usual routine, he found himself seated on a sofa alongside Harris in the dining room. He resembled a man who had been drenched due to much sexual intercourse, yet there was no trace of shame on his face. Instead, he appeared deep in thought, as if he had stumbled upon some significant revelation, akin to a great explorer who had just unearthed a momentous discovery.

In the meantime, they discussed the night's enjoyment:

"How was she? Was she a virgin? How did you spend last night?"

"Undoubtedly, she was quite untouched by anyone. I am indeed very lucky, who has got such a golden chance. I'll never forget last night. She was no less than a fairy and when I unclothed her, the dark room turned into a shining room. Aha!"

"Do you know how much money she earned for just one night? One lakh rupees, and Huda spared no effort in preparing her, working tirelessly to please her. Do you know who she was? She was the youngest daughter of a well-known minister. But I implore you, do not reveal this information under any circumstances, as it could pose a significant threat to us."

"No, I will never divulge it. Our reputation is at stake."

"Oh! I had forgotten. Please, answer quickly. Is Jesus dead or alive?"

"He's gone to hell."

With that, they parted ways.

Nine Mondays Passed

People revelled in the victory feast hosted by Harris, with numerous officers, influential figures, relatives, and friends in attendance. They engaged in discussions, deeming it a significant occasion. Harris, filled with joy and contentment, lost track of time. His supporters tirelessly sought to justify his actions against Jesus, and Harris listened intently, pleased by their efforts.

On the flip side, Jesus was strategizing his next move. Despite his economic poverty, he was spiritually affluent and morally resolute. Though physically frail, his strength of character remained unwavering. While he may have lost the case in the court of the Circle Officer, he refused to surrender his hope or faith in the justice of God. Jesus was not one to let injustice slide, determined to attain justice at any cost. He adamantly refused to accept defeat, firmly believing that justice would prevail in the end. He often reiterated this belief to his neighbours.

Jesus remarked that the path of truth was fraught with challenges. Despite this, Jesus remained committed to fighting against the injustices perpetrated by Harris. Allowing such wrongdoing to persist would only perpetuate a cycle of harm onto others in the future. Such malevolence should not be permitted to thrive, lest it corrupt society as a whole. The notion of 'might is right' contradicted the values of every civilized society; truth should reign supreme. Jesus was prepared to sacrifice everything, even his own life, in the pursuit of justice. However, Harris failed to grasp this, as he was no match for the unwavering force of truth.

Jesus remained resolute in pursuing justice and thus decided to challenge the judgment of the Circle Officer by appealing to the court of the Land Reforms Deputy Commissioner in Cester.

On a Monday morning, Jesus appeared before the commissioner's court in Cester to file his appeal. The court scheduled the first hearing for the following Saturday and summoned Harris to appear as well.

As Saturday arrived, with the unforgiving heat of June bearing down upon all, Jesus arrived at the court promptly at 7 a.m., anxiously awaiting his turn. Around 9 a.m., the Commissioner took his seat, and shortly after, Harris arrived accompanied by his legal counsel and bodyguard. Taking his place before the Commissioner, Harris sat with his legal counsel standing by his side, while Jesus waited eagerly for his turn.

After two hours passed, the Commissioner instructed his peon to summon Jesus. As Jesus entered the court and stood before him, he was promptly questioned:

"What is your relationship with Lila? Has Lila ever sold his land to anyone? And is this land currently in your possession?"

Jesus responded calmly but firmly, stating that Lila was his father and had never sold any land in his lifetime, and that Harris had forcibly seized his property.

When asked about his current residence and religion, Jesus politely informed the Commissioner that he lived in Durban and followed the Christian faith.

Aware of the social and economic disparities between Ella and Harris, the Commissioner grew irate upon hearing Jesus's account. He accused Jesus of being untrustworthy, citing a past incident of religious deception and implying further deceit in the present. Instructing Jesus to leave the court, the Commissioner and Harris remained seated on the bench.

With a smile, the Commissioner turned to Harris and asked, "What should be done?"

"Set another date," replied Harris.

Thus, the court adjourned until the following Monday.

It was an evening like any other. Birds had settled in their respective nests, but evil spirits were in search of solutions to their problems. Harris went to the Commissioner's residence to meet him. The Commissioner emerged from his inner office to welcome Harris and found a sealed envelope lying on the table. He immediately understood its significance and, without saying anything, put the envelope in a drawer and assured Harris not to worry. He dealt with such cases daily and disposed of them easily. It was not a difficult task for him; it would be resolved very soon. In the meantime, a waiter approached them and informed them that a loaded vehicle was parked at the main gate and the labourers wanted to unload it there.

Upon learning this, the Commissioner asked who the labourers were and why they wanted to unload the bags. He knew nothing about the situation and wondered what was in the vehicle.

Harris explained that he had ordered them. He instructed the labourers to unload and bring all the bags there.

The Commissioner then inquired about the contents of the bags.

Harris replied that there were five bags of basmati rice, one bag of gram, two bags of beaten paddy, two bags of sugar, and one bag of pigeon pea pulse.

For a few minutes, both men remained silent. Then, the Commissioner remarked that this was right. He would straighten Jesus out like an iron rod, ensuring he would never seek justice elsewhere again. Jesus was mad and didn't understand that he was fighting against a great man like Harris. The Commissioner said Jesus didn't realise that he could be ruined with a single fist; he was a lost man who had gone mad, but he would be taught a harsh lesson in litigation.

Harris commented that it seemed Jesus had indeed lost his mind.

The Commissioner reassured Harris not to worry. He needn't come again; the Commissioner would handle Jesus. He planned to set several dates, causing Jesus to stop attending court, and then he would deliver his decision in Harris's favour.

Harris gladly said, "Okay."

After their discussion, Harris departed from the Commissioner's residence.

The following Monday, Jesus arrived at the court of the Land Reforms Deputy Commissioner at 7 a.m. and found only a few people present. The Commissioner was also absent. As a result, Jesus wandered around, waiting for his call from the court.

He spent four hours like this, but neither the Commissioner nor Harris showed up. This left him confused about what was going on.

After some time, he approached the clerk and asked, "When will the trial begin, sir?"

The clerk responded harshly, saying, "Why are you wasting your valuable time here? Go away and come back next Monday."

Upon hearing this, Jesus left the court and headed towards Durban.

The next Monday, he returned to the same court and found both Harris and the Commissioner absent again. He approached the clerk and learned that the trial had been postponed until the following Monday. Consequently, he returned to Durban.

Jesus continued to attend court on each hearing date. In this manner, nine Mondays passed. Finally, the case was heard, and the Commissioner dismissed it.

Despite the decision, Jesus remained patient and courageous, unlike during his time at the Circle Officer's court. He said happily that this was common in office practices. He seemed transformed, as if he had gained some spiritual powers.

He declared with resolve that he would accept the challenges and take his case to the court of the Chief Commissioner in Chard. He believed he would certainly win one day. He vowed never to give up his quest for justice, stating he would expend his last drop of blood and his final breath in the pursuit of justice.

It was Tuesday when Jesus went to the Chief Commissioner in Chard to appeal. His appeal was admitted, and both parties were summoned to be present in court during the hearing.

The hearing was scheduled for Monday. Jesus arrived at Chard junction by express train a day before the hearing. As Chard was unfamiliar to him, he decided to stay in the waiting room at the junction. He had an old wallet containing fried flour, chapattis, pickles, a bowl, a jug, and a glass, ensuring he could manage his three-day journey and use these items as needed. At 10 p.m., he ate some chapattis and went to sleep.

Jesus was unaware of the misfortune awaiting him. The next morning, he woke at 6 a.m. to find that his wallet and fifty rupees from his pockets had been stolen. All his money, along with the wallet containing essential items and documents, was gone.

Realising his predicament, Jesus felt lost and disoriented for a few moments. Eventually, he gathered himself and began walking towards the Chief Commissioner's court. After a four-hour walk, he arrived at 10:30 a.m. There, he saw a legal counsel with a long white beard standing before the Chief Commissioner.

Jesus approached the clerk and asked, "When will the trial begin?"

The clerk responded brusquely, "Oh, lazy man! I called you several times, but you were absent. Were you sleeping or enjoying yourself? The trial is already in progress."

Upon hearing this, Jesus quickly entered the court and stood before the Chief Commissioner.

The Chief Commissioner asked, "Are you Jesus?"

Jesus nodded.

"Have you appealed to this court against the decision of the Land Reforms Deputy Commissioner in Cester?"

"Yes, sir!" Jesus replied.

"But you must not forget that there is a sale deed in favour of Harris.

Despite this authentic sale deed, you seek to misappropriate the land and mislead this honourable court."

Hearing this, Jesus denied the accusation, insisting that the sale deed was bogus. He explained that Harris had used his influence, connections, and wealth to fabricate the deed, leading to his wrongful victory over the truth.

The defence counsel then began his argument. He asserted that the petitioner, Jesus, was a misguided man. He claimed that Jesus had converted from Hinduism to Christianity merely to seek a better living. According to the counsel, Jesus was greedy and aimed to misappropriate land that had already been sold by his father, showing the extent of his avarice. He pointed out that Jesus lived in Durban instead of Vellore, under the influence of James, who dictated his actions.

The counsel continued, stating that individuals like Jesus posed a threat to the social harmony of the country, potentially inciting communal riots and disrupting the love and brotherhood within society. This, he argued, was a great danger to the nation.

In contrast, Harris, his client, was portrayed as an honest politician, a prosperous man, and a saviour of the poor and suffering. The counsel claimed that James was misleading Jesus to tarnish Harris's reputation.

He concluded by requesting the dismissal of the case.

Jesus wanted to say something, but as soon as he uttered the words, "Sir! I …", the court was adjourned until the following Friday.

Thus, Jesus was unable to present his legal arguments about the land, and the adjournment left him feeling nervous and frustrated.

Now wishing to return home, he began walking back to the junction. After another four-hour walk, he arrived and sat in the same waiting room where he had spent the previous night. He sat there, deep in thought, worrying about how he would make his way back to Durban.

Six Months in Jail

Jesus seemed sad for a while, spending several hours in the waiting room lost in thought as he lacked the money to buy a train ticket. Eventually, he stood up and went directly to the platform, where he found a train waiting for departure. He boarded a carriage, hoping the train would take him to Durban by the next morning.

Within an hour, the train departed, and Jesus felt a sense of relief, thinking that Durban was not far away. However, after five minutes, another passenger, offended by Jesus's old and oily clothes, forced him out of the seat. Jesus had to stand in the same carriage.

In the meantime, a Train Ticket Examiner (TTE) approached him with the police and asked to see his ticket. Jesus remained silent.

The TTE asked, "Have you got no ticket?"

Jesus still said nothing. The TTE quickly understood the situation and instructed him to follow. However, Jesus remained silent and stayed where he was.

Seeing Jesus's refusal to cooperate, the policemen became angry and beat him. Finally, they arrested him, and when the train reached Erith after a few hours, they sent him to a prison cell at the junction. At the junction, he was charged by the magistrate under various sections and penalised two thousand five hundred rupees or six months imprisonment. Since he didn't have any money to pay the penalty, he was sent to the central jail in Erith. It was there he realised that, instead of travelling on the Greenhill Express, he had boarded the Southern Express, which led to his arrest.

In the jail, Jesus was the only prisoner who didn't know Tamil, and the other prisoners were curious about the cause of his arrest. Unable to communicate, Jesus could only nod in response to their questions, which made them angry. They beat him severely, causing him to fall into an unconscious state. The Jail Superintendent then sent him to the Government Hospital in Erith.

While in the hospital, Jesus often looked at the signboard carefully and read:

OUR MOTTO:
Service
Safety
Sympathy
Moral Conduct
Cooperation
Honour
Fraternity

In the hospital, Jesus was admitted to the emergency ward. After several days, his health began to improve, and he started feeling somewhat better. The doctor then suggested a major operation on his abdomen for permanent relief, to which Jesus agreed. As he prepared for the operation, the hospital management provided him with delicious food, fruits, and milk to ensure his body was fit for the procedure. After a week of preparation, the doctor performed the operation.

Jesus felt immense gratitude towards the hospital management for their genuine care and services. He was particularly touched by the kindness and affection shown by the hospital employees, contrasting their compassion with the merciless treatment he had received from the policemen who beat him and sent him to Central Jail, Erith.

One day, Jesus found himself filled with happiness, reflecting on the kindness of some people in this world.

When the doctor visited him, Jesus expressed deep gratitude, considering the doctor a true human being unlike the jail prisoners, the Train Ticket Examiner, and the policemen. He appreciated the doctor's kindness in providing him with delicious food, medicines, fruits, and milk, acknowledging that the doctor's care had saved his life. Jesus vowed never to forget the doctor's true humanity and considered him akin to a god who had intervened to prevent his death at the hands of fellow prisoners.

After some days, Jesus regained his health, unaware that the doctor had secretly removed his kidney to sell at a high price for profit. Jesus thanked the doctor, believing he was being sent back to the prison cell to serve the remaining period of his arrest.

His days in prison were filled with suffering, and he often found himself reflecting on his past. Sometimes he struggled to maintain patience, while at other times he felt a sense of assurance. He drew strength from the story of Job's suffering and eventual recovery, eagerly awaiting the day when he would be free from the confines of the jail. Eventually, after six long months, that day arrived, and he was released.

Upon his release, Jesus looked back at the Black Hall where he had been imprisoned and asked the Jail Superintendent how he would manage to return home without a penny to his name. The Superintendent coldly informed him that the black seal on his hand signified that he was being released after completing his "jail march", which would facilitate his journey home.

Hearing this, Jesus wasted no time and hurried towards the paths leading to the junction, determined never to look back. After several hours of walking, he reached the junction, but now he proceeded cautiously. He approached an inquiry office and asked, "Sir, which train is departing for Durban?"

Fortunately, as Jesus asked, he heard an announcement from the inquiry office, "The South-East Express, train number 21441, standing on platform 2, will depart for Worcester shortly. Passengers are requested to take their seats with their proper train tickets."

Quickly, he dashed to the platform, entered a second-class carriage, and found a seat. With this, his fear subsided momentarily, though the thought of having no ticket lingered in his mind, raising concerns about the possibility of being arrested again. To reassure himself, he glanced at the black seal on his hand, a mark left by the jail administration. Whenever the Train Ticket Examiner approached, Jesus displayed the seal, prompting the examiner to move on without questioning him further.

During the journey, Jesus reflected on various aspects of life and humanity. He recalled how he had rationed thirteen loaves of chapatti during his time in jail, using one loaf each day to stave off hunger. Many thoughts and emotions flooded his mind, pondering the injustices he had endured and the struggles faced by the poor in society, including himself. He questioned whether he had made any mistakes and contemplated the actions of influential figures like Harris, whose behaviour had impacted his life profoundly.

Finally, he muttered to himself, "If winter comes, can spring be far behind? How pleasant it is to experience spring after enduring winter's hardships!"

After a long journey of twenty-four hours, Jesus anticipated reaching Durban, unaware of the challenges that lay ahead in his life.

Resurrection

During the six months, Jesus remained absent from his home. Despite their efforts, his neighbours were unable to locate him, leaving them feeling helpless and reluctant. Meanwhile, the responsibility of caring for Leo and Luca fell upon them. They diligently looked after Jesus's children, who felt hopeless and feared their father might never return. At times, they wept bitterly, longing for their father and reminiscing about their mother. Their situation grew dire at times, with days passing without food as they mourned the absence of their parents. In their despair, they contemplated the justice of God and the role of fate in their lives.

The people of Vellore were aware of Jesus's disappearance, prompting them to convene a village meeting for discussion. In this meeting, they decided to perform his death rites in accordance with Hindu customs, as Jesus had been a Hindu before. Collecting donations from the entire village, they purchased a costly shroud for him. However, since his dead body had not been found, they crafted an effigy out of straw and adorned it with the expensive shroud.

The bier, made of green bamboo, was then carried on the shoulders of villagers from Jesus's birthplace to the village crematorium, where Emily had also been cremated. Thousands of people participated in the funeral march, a testament to the community's respect and regard for Jesus. Upon reaching the crematorium, they erected a pyre and placed the effigy upon it.

As the priest stood near the mouth of the effigy on the northern side, he began to chant the holy mouth-fire hymn. According to Hindu tradition, it was essential for a man of the Dome caste to perform the ritual of placing holy fire into the mouth of the effigy. This ritual was believed to secure a place for the soul of the deceased in heaven. People held firm beliefs that when a mouth-fire was offered in this manner, the soul of the deceased would ascend to heaven.

After completing the cremation ritual, the mourners circled the pyre five times, each time placing at least one sacred wood onto the fire. This traditional act marked the completion of Jesus's cremation, bringing a sense of fulfilment to those present. They proudly declared that they had fulfilled their social responsibilities in honouring Jesus's memory.

The following day, they gathered for another meeting to plan additional rituals related to Jesus's death, as per societal customs. For the rituals of the tenth day, they invited paternal priests and generously donated various items. These offerings included a cushioned bed, a sofa set, a cushion, a bed sheet, a pillow, a warm cushion, one quintal of basmati rice, a cow, and one thousand and fifty-one rupees. These offerings were intended to be sent to Jesus's spirit in the next spiritual world, ensuring that his spirit could live peacefully and joyfully near the heavenly seat of God.

During Jesus's death feast, the community arranged a customary meal, adhering to tradition. They prepared six hundred litres of curd, eleven varieties of sweets, and eleven types of vegetables, symbolizing their respect and homage to Jesus. The feast was attended by the majority of Vellore's residents, as well as others from surrounding areas. Participants left feeling joyful and satisfied after partaking in the communal meal.

On the third day of the feast, they convened another meeting to assess the management of the event. Once again, they were filled with happiness upon learning that their efforts had been extraordinary. The successful execution of the feast further reinforced their sense of unity and solidarity as a community, serving as a fitting tribute to Jesus's memory.

The community members were elated with the success of the death feast management. They applauded each other, expressing their satisfaction that despite the grandeur of the event, they had only spent seventy-seven thousand rupees. They believed that their extensive efforts, even after Jesus's passing, would ensure his soul's ascension to heaven, granting him eternal peace and rest.

The success of the death feast was underscored by the participation of hundreds of Brahmins among the thousands of attendees. It was widely believed that if more than a hundred Brahmins partook in the feast, the soul of the deceased would undoubtedly reside in heaven. Furthermore, the unexpected presence of Harris, Jesus's erstwhile enemy, was seen as a sign that their enmity had ceased. Harris's active involvement, including consuming eleven porridges in eleven plates, was interpreted as confirmation that his soul would also find peace and rest in heaven.

In the end, they deemed Jesus fortunate, as even his enemy had attended his death feast, ensuring his soul's journey to the heavenly abode.

Harris expressed deep regret over Jesus's untimely demise during the death feast, acknowledging it as the inevitable law of nature. He praised Jesus, referring to him as a "good man" and equating him to Jesus Christ. Harris reminisced about their close relationship and recounted instances where Jesus and his wife had assisted him, who had diligently served as cooks during his election campaigns. Overcome with emotion, Harris lamented Jesus's passing, expressing disbelief and sorrow.

The villagers, echoing Harris's sentiments, took pride in Jesus's presumed place in heaven. They believed that by honouring him in death, they had fulfilled their responsibilities, even if they had not fully shared in his sorrows during his lifetime. They found solace in the belief that enmity between Harris and Jesus ceased with the latter's departure from this world.

In a subsequent meeting on the fourth day, they decided to deposit the remaining funds from Jesus's death feast with the society's treasurer. This amount would be reserved for future use, specifically for expenses related to another member's death. This decision reflected their commitment to supporting one another in need, even beyond the scope of Jesus's passing.

They were ecstatic and said that they had thousands of rupees in their treasury, which was enough for another death feast for a poor or helpless person.

In contrast, the entire city of Durban was plunged into deep distress because of Jesus's disappearance. The people of Durban were convinced that Jesus was dead since they had not seen him for six months. Therefore, they called a meeting in the town hall and decided to perform his death rites in a very simple manner. After the meeting, they planned to hold a condolence gathering for his untimely death. They stood up in rows for the ceremony. In the meantime, Harris arrived uninvited and joined them in the first row to take part.

Firstly, James began to address the condolence meeting and said, "We express deep sorrow for his untimely death – for the passing of a man who was a paragon of truth and honesty. We pray to the Almighty for peace and rest for Jesus's immortal soul, and for strength for his kinsmen so they may find peace and solace in their lives."

Harris also paid tribute to Jesus. He said, "It is a matter of deep sorrow that Jesus is no longer with us in this mortal world. He was indeed very honest, polite, and truthful. He never tried to hurt anyone in his life. A man like him should not have died. It is truly my loss. I feel profound sorrow for his death, but we are now helpless in the hands of the Almighty. We can do nothing because we are unable to bring him back from heaven. He is now surely in heaven, not in hell. Oh … Oh! A man like him, I have never seen in my life, and now he is in heaven and will never return to me or us. We express deep sorrow for his untimely death and pray to the Almighty for peace and rest for his soul and for strength for his kinsmen so that they can more easily face this profound sorrow."

Harris's eyes were streaming with tears, dampening his Gandhi coat, the Gandhi cap in his right hand which he was using to wipe his tears, his dhoti, and his shirt. After paying tribute, he stood in the front row to participate in the condolence meeting. Everyone in each row remained silent, closing their eyes for two minutes of prayer, seeking peace for Jesus's soul and strength for his kinsmen.

Harris's bodyguard stood beside the rows, keeping an eye on him. At that moment, he saw Jesus approaching through a narrow street. The bodyguard quickly went to Harris and nudged him. When Harris opened his eyes, the bodyguard indicated that Jesus was coming and he saw Jesus himself.

Seeing Jesus, Harris was struck with astonishment, feeling as if a sea of shame had engulfed him. He swiftly left the place, got into his marvellous car, and drove towards Chester. After two minutes of concentration, the people opened their eyes to find Harris gone and Jesus standing before them. They were astonished to see Jesus.

James quickly approached him, shook his hand, and exclaimed, "Jesus is indeed Jesus! Jesus Christ! It is indeed a resurrection."

The condolence meeting transformed into a joyful gathering. Their hearts filled with joy at the sight of Jesus, believing his arrival to be a resurrection. They declared the event to be extraordinary and enjoyed it wholeheartedly. Embracing one another, their faith in the Almighty was strengthened. They remarked that such a marvellous event rarely happens in the world, considering it a miracle that Jesus arrived just as they were holding a condolence meeting. It was indeed wonderful, and Jesus remained a mystery to them. They observed that unusual events always seemed to happen to Jesus, and they began to believe he was a wonder who would perform divine works.

There was a sense of uncontrollable pleasure, and they could not hide their happiness. Some among them criticised Harris, expressing their bitterness towards him. Some said that if he were present, they would have kicked him and taken revenge for his exploitation, suppression, and atrocities.

In their joy, they exclaimed, "Oh, Harris! Where did Harris go? When did he leave? Was he Judas?"

But no one answered, and everyone ran to Jesus. The atmosphere of distress transformed into unexpected bliss, akin to the arrival of rain in the summer.

Jesus was surprised to learn about the condolence meeting held for him and was speechless for a while. Smiling, he said, "Oh my God!"

He had no words to say anything more and seemed puzzled. People asked him about his experiences, and he narrated all the events that had happened to him in detail. They apologised for holding the condolence meeting.

After his return, people began to say, "Jesus is indeed Jesus! Jesus Christ! He will work only for the betterment of mankind and will bring divine bliss to this dim and dry world, replacing miseries and toils."

With Jesus's arrival, there was an atmosphere of contentment in Durban. In contrast, there was an atmosphere of misery and toil in Harris's palace, where the events were a major topic of discussion. Harris was nervous.

Some people said that Harris had not made any mistakes because it was crucial for him to participate in the event to garner support from those individuals for the imminent election. Someone also mentioned that he shouldn't have left the condolence meeting secretly because when others opened their eyes, they were eagerly searching for him, wanting to catch a glimpse of him as if he were a resurrected figure like Jesus. At home, Harris sat silently on the sofa, resembling a tired soldier.

Hearing all this, he felt ashamed and wanted to justify his actions. He explained that he was in deep distress and that he hadn't left the place intentionally, but rather automatically and unknowingly. At that moment, he couldn't understand why his legs started moving. When his supporters asked him about it, he told them everything. He admitted that he became nervous and, as he was getting into the car, he once fell to the ground. Huda helped him up, allowing him to take his seat in the car. He also mentioned that fifty-five thousand rupees, which he had donated for the people of Vellore to celebrate Jesus's death feast, went to waste. He asked them not to share this information with anyone.

It was Monday, the first day of Jesus's return to Durban after more than six months. Jesus was sleeping when the police arrived and arrested him. He was taken to Cester Police Station, where he asked the reason for his arrest. Instead of answering, the police beat him and told him, "You will know everything in detail in jail." Finally, the police sent him to the Divisional Jail in Cester.

The next morning, his neighbours went to Cester Police Station to find out the reason for his arrest. They discovered that there was a non-bailable warrant against him issued by the court of the District Judge in Cester. This warrant had been filed by Harris due to Jesus's non-payment of twenty thousand rupees as compensation, plus two thousand rupees as costs, along with twelve per cent interest on that amount from the date of the case's resolution in the court of the Circle Officer, Cester, following the dismissal of Jesus's appeal in the court of the Chief Commissioner, Chard.

That same day, a bail petition was submitted on Jesus's behalf in the Lower Court, but it was rejected. However, his neighbours were determined not to let him remain in jail, especially as he had only just returned after more than six months. Therefore, another bail petition was submitted on Jesus's behalf before the Chief Justice of the High Court, Chard. This time, his bail petition was granted, and he was released from jail.

Soon after the release, Jesus fell ill at his home. He was, therefore, admitted to the Government Hospital, Cester. But despite his regular treatment for a week, he couldn't recover. His physical health and his physical condition continued to deteriorate. He was, therefore, sent to the Edwin Hospital, Malabar for further treatment where a sonologist investigated that the cause of his intolerable pain was an infection on the right side of his renal area and his one kidney had been removed. After a major operation, the doctor took out the infected part and he became well. After recovering his health, he was discharged from the hospital and returned home. In Durban he combined his daily duties with his duty as a gardener at St Xavier School, Durban. But he was puzzled as to "how his right kidney was lost."

On the contrary, Jesus was resolute in seeking justice for the injustice perpetrated by Harris. Consequently, he bid farewell to his quandary and resolved to venture forth to ascertain the current status of the case.

It was a Tuesday when Jesus proceeded to the precincts of the civil court in Cester to seek legal counsel regarding his next course of action. There, he encountered a barrister who advised him to initiate a fresh case against Harris under relevant sections of criminal law. Acting upon this advice, Jesus lodged a new case against Harris before the Civil Judge of Cester. The case was accepted, and both parties were summoned to appear before the court.

After several months, the trial commenced with representatives from both the defence and the prosecution in attendance.

The prosecution counsel implored the Judge to consider the noble character of his client, Jesus, contrasted with the accused, Harris, who wielded significant influence. Harris had orchestrated a fraudulent sale deed to unlawfully appropriate Jesus's land. Jesus, being a man of integrity, was hesitant to confront Harris unnecessarily. Harris, a wealthy individual, owned substantial estates in New Delhi, Erith, and Cester, and operated Bright Finance and Company Limited, a non-banking entity. Leveraging his affluence and authority, Harris oppressed an upstanding individual like Jesus.

It was highlighted that Jesus's father, Lila, had never sold any of his land, making the signatures on the sale deed spurious. The purported introducers had provided an affidavit admitting to the falsity of their signatures. Furthermore, the thumb impression of Lila was deemed counterfeit, a fact that could be verified by comparing it to the imprint on his old ration card. This evidence strongly indicated the fraudulent nature of the sale deed obtained by Harris. Consequently, the prosecution implored the Judge to convict Harris on various charges.

Upon hearing the prosecution's arguments, the defence counsel, a distinguished advocate from the High Court in Chard, vigorously defended his client, Harris, fulfilling his duty by presenting compelling arguments in his favour.

He asserted that Harris, an honest and benevolent individual, was renowned for his generosity and leadership within the New Socialist Party, dedicating himself to the welfare of the underprivileged. It was inconceivable, he argued, that Harris would engage in fraudulent activities such as obtaining a bogus sale deed. The defence contended that James, by accusing Harris, was motivated by political agendas and a desire to seize land that had already been legitimately sold by Lila, Jesus's father.

Furthermore, the defence portrayed Jesus as driven by greed, suggesting that his conversion to Christianity from Hinduism was solely for monetary gain, aiming to amass wealth. According to Harris, Jesus lacked direction and sought to lead others astray. He claimed that Lila had indeed sold the land, receiving sixty thousand rupees through a cheque from the State Bank of India, which was duly encashed before the land transaction took place. The defence maintained that the sale deed was legitimate and had been properly registered with the Registrar's office in Cester. Consequently, the land rightfully belonged to Harris.

In light of these arguments, the defence counsel pleaded for the dismissal of the case against Harris and proposed that Jesus be convicted under section 211 of the Indian Penal Code for false charges.

The Judge listened attentively to the proceedings and made the decision to scrutinize the affidavit, thumb impression, and bank records. Consequently, he adjourned the court for the following day.

On the subsequent day, a specialist in thumb impressions and signatures was present in court. After comparing and verifying the signatures and thumb impression, the specialist concluded that significant disparities existed between the signatures on the sale deed and the affidavit. Additionally, it was determined that the thumb impression of Lila on the sale deed was indeed counterfeit. Upon reading the specialist's report, the Judge displayed visible dismay, casting a meaningful glance towards Harris before adjourning the court once again.

Later that evening, Harris, accompanied by his elder brother who served as the Minister for Appointments in the Central Government, visited the Judge at his residence. Although neither brother broached the subject of the ongoing case, upon learning of the visitor's identity, the Judge recognized the opportunity to extend a favour.

The Judge reassured Harris, minimizing the significance of the fraudulent sale deed, emphasizing that Jesus would gain nothing from it. He pointed out another compelling argument against Jesus, indicating that he would ultimately be the loser, while Harris would emerge as the victor. The Judge conveyed this sentiment firmly.

Upon hearing the Judge's words, Harris was elated and expressed his gratitude. He acknowledged the matter as one of his family's honour rather than merely a property issue. Harris pledged his unwavering support to the Judge, offering assistance whenever needed. He also mentioned that his sons were currently unemployed, indicating his willingness to help them secure employment, leveraging his familial connections within the employment department.

The Judge, upon learning of Harris's offer, expressed profound gratitude, acknowledging it as a significant act of kindness. He confessed his embarrassment regarding his sons' unemployment despite their academic achievements. He appealed for a solution to their predicament, as they had already surpassed the maximum age limit for government employment.

In this exchange, both Harris and the Judge found common ground, each offering support and assistance to the other in their respective challenges.

Harris reassured the Judge that age would not be an obstacle for him, and he promised to fulfil the formalities for the appointment retroactively. He emphasized that age was irrelevant for someone of his stature, indicating his confidence in resolving the Judge's employment-related concerns swiftly.

The Judge listened intently, unable to contain his joy. He affectionately addressed Harris as his dearest, expressing gratitude for the prospect of resolving his longstanding issue. The Judge revealed that once the problem was resolved, he anticipated receiving substantial dowries for his children, which he planned to encash for at least one crore rupees each during the upcoming wedding season. He confessed that currently, nobody approached him regarding their children's marriages, leading him to feel emotional as he reflected on his situation.

In this heartfelt exchange, the Judge found solace in Harris's assurance and looked forward to resolving his financial difficulties, while Harris reaffirmed his commitment to assisting the Judge and his family.

The Judge, momentarily lost in thought about his sons, expressed regret over their unmarried status, realizing they had been of marriageable age for 47 years without any prospects. Quickly returning his attention to the courtroom, he apologized for his lapse and assured Harris of a resolution to his employment matter within a week.

The trial resumed on Thursday with all parties present, and both counsels presented their arguments over the subsequent four days.

Following multiple hearings, the Judge delivered his verdict. He noted that the sale deed had been registered with the registrar's office long ago, and the plaintiff had not contested it until now. Consequently, as the land was in Harris's possession, there was no basis for objection against the sale deed. With the stroke of his pen and the official seal of the court, the case was dismissed, and the court's order took effect.

A Man of Mercy

Despite the setback of the Lower Court's judgment, Jesus remained steadfast in his pursuit of justice. He deliberated on the case and the flaws in the justice system for several days. After careful consideration, he resolved to appeal to the High Court in Chard, determined not to let injustice prevail.

After saving over ten thousand and five hundred rupees and borrowing an additional thousand, Jesus embarked on his journey from Durban to Chard by express train. Arriving at his destination late in the evening, he found himself unfamiliar with the area and opted to spend the night in the waiting room of the station.

He arrived at the waiting room. He ate the chapatti he had brought from home. He was very alert and decided not to sleep that night. Therefore, he continued to watch the television, which was already on in the waiting room, for the entire night, unable to close his eyes even for a moment.

The night brought new experiences – a night when he had to stay awake and alert. Occasionally, he began to drift off. Sometimes, he was on the verge of succumbing to drowsiness and felt uneasy. But he fought hard to stay alert. Somehow, he managed to endure the tough ordeal. He continued to mutter verses from religious texts throughout the night. Some people thought he was mad for not sleeping, but only he knew the reason behind his actions. He often remembered the night when he had lost everything. And so, the night passed.

Fate seemed to be pursuing him – or perhaps time was pursuing him. He remained vigilant in the waiting room that night, but he was about to fall prey to another unwelcome situation, entirely beyond his control and awareness. In the meantime, it seemed he was shaped by time, driven by time, and existed for a time.

The next morning, he got up and refreshed himself. After performing the necessary ablutions, he headed towards the roads leading to the High Court. When he arrived, he stood by the main gate.

In the meantime, a passerby was walking along the way. Jesus approached him and asked where the Advocate's Hall was. The stranger offered to guide him, mentioning he would take him to an excellent advocate who was honest, polite, cooperative, and kind. This advocate was especially good for those who were poor and helpless.

Jesus asked the stranger for the advocate's seat number. He replied that it was number one. Jesus then inquired if the stranger knew him personally. The stranger confirmed that he did, affirming the advocate's honesty and adding that Jesus was very fortunate to have come to him first. He assured Jesus that he would certainly win his case.

Within ten minutes, they reached the advocate. Seeing a client so early made the advocate very happy, as he anticipated a profitable day. He smiled warmly and thanked the stranger who had brought Jesus to him, even giving him a hundred rupee note to buy sweets as a token of gratitude for helping Jesus.

The advocate then asked Jesus, "What's the matter?"

Jesus expressed his predicament respectfully, explaining that he was a very poor man, utterly unable to withstand the powerful influence of Harris, who was oppressing him. Harris was a Member of Parliament, a very wealthy and influential man. He was using his might and wealth to suppress Jesus, and it would be a great mercy if the advocate could help him in such a critical situation. Jesus said he needed the advocate's cooperation, and if he did not receive it, there was no one else who would help him, and he feared he would soon perish.

The advocate showed compassion and assured Jesus that he would alleviate his suffering. He confidently stated that Jesus would undoubtedly win the case. He also mentioned that he was the only advocate in that court who truly helped the poor and helpless. All the other advocates were cunning and driven solely by money – they spoke for money, acted for money, thought about money, saluted for money, and worked for money. According to him, he worked only for the sake of people like Jesus. He urged Jesus not to forget the principles he had shared.

Jesus, having spent most of his life in the village, could not recognise the potential deceit and manipulation of the advocate. He began to trust him completely, believing that the advocate was no less than a godsend for someone as suffering and poor as himself.

Saying this, Jesus laid all the documents on the table before the advocate. As he did so, the advocate said, "All is well. Now place one thousand and one rupees on the documents."

Jesus took the amount from his wallet and put it on the documents.

Within five minutes, the advocate reviewed the documents and handed Jesus an advocate nomination slip to sign. Jesus signed it, and the advocate then instructed his clerk to collect twenty thousand rupees as his fee.

Hearing this, Jesus looked around in confusion. He said, "But, sir, I have only brought ten thousand rupees."

The clerk replied, "What? Sir, deposit the fee first. Then we can discuss further."

Jesus steadied himself and thought about the money he had with him. He remained silent, contemplating his next step, as he didn't have the full amount. He appeared puzzled for a few moments, considering the matter seriously.

Suddenly, he spoke up, "But sir, I gave you one thousand rupees just a moment ago."

The advocate replied that it was merely a token gesture, just to touch the documents, and told him to understand the situation.

Jesus said he understood but reiterated that he had only brought ten thousand rupees.

The advocate reassured him, saying it was fine and to give him the money he had now.

Handing over the money, Jesus explained that he wouldn't be able to return to Durban as he didn't have a single penny left for the fare or to buy toffees for his sons – the fare to Chard was forty rupees.

Seeing his predicament, the clerk gave him forty rupees and told him to pay the remaining fee as soon as possible.

Jesus promised to pay the remaining amount in due time and requested just ten rupees to buy some toffees for his sons. The advocate loudly remarked that toffees were very harmful to children's teeth.

Jesus acknowledged this and left the office, walking to the junction where he boarded the train. It was Sunday when Jesus finally reached home. Upon his arrival, John and Joy eagerly pounced on him, asking for toffees. This made him deeply sad, and he couldn't speak a word for a few moments.

After a while, he spoke in a sorrowful tone, "Oh my dear children, I had no money, so I couldn't buy toffees for you. I will go to the market in the evening and buy some for you, I promise."

However, the children didn't calm down and began to roll on the ground, creating a pathetic scene. Somehow, he managed to gather them into his lap. Eventually, he went to the village shop and bought toffees for them.

The next day, he resumed his duties as a gardener, but was dissatisfied because he still needed to pay the outstanding amount to the advocate in the High Court. So, in the evening, he approached some traders seeking another job, but he couldn't find any. Despite this setback, he persisted, and after a few days, he secured a job as a night guard on a trader's farm.

Each day, he rose at dawn, washed clothes and dishes, cooked food, and got John and Joy ready for school. Then he left home to perform his duties at St Xavier School, Durban. Every evening, he cooked dinner for his children before heading to his night guard job, carrying a long, sturdy wooden rod in his right hand and a torch in his left. This became his daily routine, which he maintained for several months.

Three months passed this way. He continued both jobs, working tirelessly to save the money needed to pay the advocate. Determined not to delay any longer, he left Durban for Chard to settle the debt. Arriving at the junction late at night, he spent the night in the same waiting room where he had stayed before. There was a constant announcement warning passengers to beware of pickpockets, as more than a dozen complaints had been recorded within the past twenty-four hours. Jesus remained vigilant to avoid becoming a victim. Despite his tiredness, he couldn't sleep for even a moment.

The next morning, he refreshed himself and walked towards the advocate's residence. After a few minutes, he arrived at the advocate's home. The advocate, who was brushing his teeth, stopped when he saw Jesus and sat in his wheelchair. They began to converse.

"O Jesus! You great fool! Are you still alive? Did you forget to come here and pay my fee? Have you brought the money or not?"

"Yes, sir!"

"Give it to me quickly. Why are you waiting? Hand it over."

Jesus took out an old handkerchief from his worn wallet and began to untie the bundles of money, which were covered with flour. He then carefully arranged and counted the sum several times.

After counting, he said, "Rupees ten thousand and forty only."

The advocate, eager to take the money as he needed to go to court and was still brushing his teeth, grew impatient. He became angry and said that if Jesus intended to pay, he should do so immediately, rather than just showing the money.

Jesus apologised for the delay in counting and extended his hand with the money.

The advocate, annoyed, extended both his hands and said, "Give it to me, otherwise go away."

Understanding the urgency, Jesus handed over the sum, dropping the money, both notes and coins, into the advocate's hands.

Thanking him for the money, the advocate grumbled, "What's all this? Is this money? One rupee! Two rupees! It will take years to count. Fine. All right. Go away."

Taking the money, the advocate put it in the drawer and gave Jesus his contact number, which Jesus noted down. The advocate then shifted into his professional demeanour, behaving differently from before. Jesus noticed that the advocate, who had previously spoken very kindly, was now acting more formally. The advocate told him not to visit without an appointment and assured him that he would be informed about the progress of the case. Within a few minutes, Jesus was dismissed and left the office.

Fate, however, remained unfavourable to him, refusing to allow him any peace or rest. Unbeknownst to Jesus, he was about to be caught in another unfortunate turn of events. Despite this, he felt relieved that he had paid the advocate and believed that justice would soon be served. As he walked towards the railway junction, he thought about his situation, sometimes voicing his thoughts aloud. He moved with a sense of hope, expecting that justice would soon be granted to him.

After some time, he reached the junction and purchased a ticket for an express train scheduled to depart in half an hour. Feeling hungry, he bought some guavas to eat. After eating just one guava, he collapsed to the ground, where he remained unconscious for several hours.

Eventually, the police arrived and took him to a nearby hospital. Two days later, Jesus regained consciousness. When he opened his eye and realised he was in a hospital, he felt a mix of relief and confusion.

Seeing this, the doctor noted that Jesus was shivering. Jesus, trembling, asked why his left eye was covered and only his right eye could see. He wanted to know what had happened to his left eye and where he was. Was he in a hospital? Was the person with him a doctor? Was he okay? Why was he there?

The doctor sternly told him to stay quiet and not to speak loudly, as it could be very harmful. He explained that Jesus had been found unconscious at the junction, and the police had brought him in for treatment. When he arrived, his left eye was bleeding, and despite their efforts, they couldn't save the sight in that eye. If Jesus wanted more information, he would have to inquire at the police station.

Jesus closed his eyes and mouth, trying to process this information. After some time, he asked again what had happened to his left eye and if he was now a one-eyed man.

The doctor, frustrated, left his chair, approached Jesus, and angrily asked if he wanted to save his right eye or not. He warned Jesus to stay silent, or he risked losing his remaining sight and becoming completely blind.

Terrified, Jesus kept silent, closed his remaining eye, and stayed in the hospital for the next ten days. He eventually recovered physically, though with the loss of one eye, and never learned the exact reason for his injury.

On the eleventh day, he was discharged. He left the hospital, sat on the ground outside, and pondered his next steps. He reflected on the motto he had read on a yellow board in the hospital:

OUR COMMITMENT:

Your long life
Your organs' safety
Your free-of-cost treatment
Your quick recovery
Your healthy life

He remained sitting there for about seven hours. Suddenly, he stood up and began walking towards Durban, as he had no money for a bus or train fare and lacked the courage to travel without a ticket. Along the way, he sought refuge in churches, temples, gurudwaras, and mosques, gratefully accepting any food offered by the local people. During this journey, he became a symbol of mercy, embodying and relying on the kindness of others.

To avoid falling victim to sectarian violence, Jesus adapted to the customs and religions of each village he passed through. In Muslim villages, he presented himself as a Muslim; in Christian villages, as a Christian; in Sikh villages, as a Sikh; and in Hindu villages, as a Hindu. He did this not out of deceit but as a means of self-preservation, understanding that identifying with the locals' faith would protect him from harm.

His intentions were pure, and although he had to lie about his identity, it was never to cause harm but to ensure his safety. Jesus was acutely aware that presenting himself as a fellow believer would eliminate any risk of hostility from the villagers. This necessity led him to change not only his religion but also his name, village to village, according to the predominant faith of the inhabitants. He later reflected that he had lied three hundred times during his week-long journey – not to deceive, but to protect himself from the brutal reality of extremism and sectarianism.

As Jesus entered his home in Durban, instead of rushing to greet him, John and Joy seemed to avoid him, distancing themselves. They didn't rush for toffees or eagerly seek his lap as they used to. His heart sank at their apparent rejection. He stood in silence, enveloped in a mix of confusion, affection, love, and compassion, feeling utterly lost in the midst of his own family's rejection.

After a few moments, Jesus mustered the courage to call out to them, "Come here, my dears – my children – come to me."

But they responded coldly, "Leave our home."

Jesus tried to reason with them, insisting that he was their father.

However, they remained unmoved, accusing him of being a thief and demanding to know where his left eye was. They refused to acknowledge him as their father, dismissing him as a one-eyed stranger trying to deceive them. The situation was heartbreaking for Jesus, as he stood there, rejected by his own children, all because he had lost an eye in pursuit of justice.

Feeling utterly disregarded and helpless, Jesus was overcome with nervousness. He couldn't find the words to express his sorrow. He felt like a stranger in his own home, abandoned by his own children simply because he had sacrificed part of himself in the pursuit of justice. It seemed as though he was destined to be an alien in this world, and eventually, he would depart from it, leaving behind everything except his virtues.

Meanwhile, John and Joy sought help from their neighbours to remove Jesus from their home. Soon, a group of people arrived and found Jesus sitting on the ground, with both hands on his head, visibly distressed.

Filled with shame at the sight, they listened to his tragic story. Eventually, they confirmed to John and Joy that indeed, he was their father – the same loving father who had always showered them with treats. They reassured the children that despite his loss, Jesus would continue to care for them. Though he had lost his left eye, they expressed gratitude that he was still alive, thanks to the grace of God.

May I Beat You?

On one hand, Jesus returned home, looking forward to spending the night with his children. On the other hand, unbeknownst to him, Harris had been keeping a close eye on Jesus's movements through his secret informants. Upon Jesus's return, Harris promptly learned of it and, exploiting his influence within the police department, decided to have Jesus arrested.

Jesus, blissfully unaware of Harris's machinations, found solace in the company of his children, hoping for a peaceful and restful night. He never imagined that he would once again face arrest and lose his newfound happiness.

As night fell, the very same day Jesus returned from Chard, nursing the loss of his left eye, he slept peacefully alongside his children. However, their tranquillity was abruptly shattered when police personnel arrived at their doorstep. Jesus, roused from his slumber, answered the door to find them standing there.

The officers, addressing him as the "one-eyed man," questioned whether he had returned from Chard and whether he was alive or dead. They asked the whereabouts of his left eye in a mocking tone. They informed him that a seat awaited him in jail, as the jailer had extended an invitation. They instructed him to accompany them and take his place in the police van parked nearby – a vehicle recently purchased by the department. They sarcastically remarked that he would be the first accused to occupy the vehicle, dubbing him "lucky number one." They insinuated that he could easily guess why they had chosen the new vehicle for his transport, hinting at further humiliation awaiting him at the police station.

In this manner, they sought to degrade him in his own home before effecting his arrest.

Jesus, completely unaware of the reason behind his arrest, calmly inquired about the cause from the police officers. However, they remained silent, likely under the influence of Harris. Despite Jesus's gentle persistence, they refused to provide an answer, and he was ultimately arrested.

The officers, addressing him disdainfully as "a one-eyed man," ordered him to take his seat immediately, promising that all his questions would be answered at the police station, where their rods would serve as the ultimate arbitrators. They boasted about the new wooden sticks supplied by the department, claiming they were specially trained to use them to extract confessions. This psychological torment continued as they displayed the slim sticks in their hands, asserting their ability to extract information from any accused.

Finally, they questioned Jesus, asking if he understood the situation. His heart pounding with fear, Jesus was unable to conceal his anxiety. However, they admonished him not to feign ignorance and instructed him to follow them, leaving his sleeping children behind. Despite his inner turmoil, Jesus complied, taking his place in the police vehicle as instructed.

Arriving at the police station, Jesus noticed a large signboard proudly displaying the station's motto. He read the half-red and half-blue signboard repeatedly, absorbing its message carefully:

WE COMMIT:

Politeness
Obedience
Co-operation
Loyalty
Security
Courtesy
Efficiency

Upon reading the beautifully painted words on the signboard, Jesus felt a surge of optimism. He believed that this police station would be different, free from the injustices he had endured throughout his life. He hoped that the police would treat him fairly and assist him in his quest for justice. Feeling patient and at ease, he held onto this hope.

However, his optimism quickly faded when the police approached him. They accused him of becoming a litigant, claiming that his sole purpose was to fabricate charges against Harris in order to tarnish his reputation. They suggested that he had been misled by James and other Christians into pursuing these false accusations.

This sudden turn of events shattered Jesus's hopes and left him disillusioned. He had hoped for assistance from the police, but instead, he was met with accusations and scepticism. Uncertain of how to proceed, Jesus found himself caught between his desire for justice and the accusations being hurled against him.

The policemen continued their tirade against Jesus, painting him as a troublemaker who frequented courts and advocates with no purpose other than to cause trouble. They accused James of inciting him, suggesting that Jesus, in his alleged aimlessness, had converted from Hinduism to Christianity. According to them, he was unfairly defaming Harris, a Member of Parliament whom they portrayed as an honest benefactor of the poor. They claimed Jesus sought to reclaim land once sold by his father, branding him as dishonest and warning him that he would never be released from jail if he persisted.

The officers warned Jesus about the intricacies of police tactics, insinuating that they could manipulate the legal system to keep him incarcerated indefinitely. They advised him to consider his options carefully, implying that his continued defiance would result in a life spent behind bars. Their words were intended as a stern warning to Jesus, suggesting that he rethink his actions and the potential consequences thereof.

Jesus vehemently refuted the accusations levelled against him, asserting his innocence and the baselessness of the charges. He explained that Harris had unlawfully seized a small portion of land, compelling him to convert to Christianity for support when his own community failed to come to his aid. He reminded them of the Christian Society's assistance during his time of need, contrasting it with the indifference of his own society.

Jesus expressed disbelief at the notion that he, a humble man, could ever entertain thoughts of defaming someone as influential as Harris. He highlighted Harris's power and influence, suggesting that the authorities were better equipped to comprehend it than he was. He also dispelled the notion that his father had ever sold their land, denouncing it as a grave injustice.

Despite his vulnerability and poverty, Jesus maintained his unwavering faith in the power of truth. He acknowledged his own limitations but emphasized the ultimate authority of truth, confident that it would prevail in due time. He urged patience, believing that the truth would eventually come to light, bringing justice to his situation.

Horrified by the brutality inflicted upon Jesus, his neighbours visited the police station seeking answers. To their dismay, they found Jesus grievously injured, his face stained with blood and his clothes soaked in crimson. Witnessing his suffering, they were filled with outrage and disbelief.

Meanwhile, a callous constable taunted Jesus, labelling him a troublemaker and warning him of further consequences if he dared to pursue litigation in the future. His callous remarks only served to deepen the sense of despair among the onlookers.

As they reflected on the injustice unfolding before them, the bystanders lamented the harsh reality of their society, where might triumphed over right and the vulnerable were left to suffer. They despaired over the lack of compassion and justice in a world that seemed to favour the powerful over the helpless.

Their despair was compounded as they glanced at a signboard hanging behind the Police Sub-Inspector's chair, its red and blue hues offering a stark contrast to the grim reality of their circumstances.

MAY I HELP YOU?

People voiced their discontent, suggesting the sign should read "MAY I BEAT YOU?" instead, reflecting the brutality they had witnessed.

In response to complaints from Jesus's neighbours, high-level police officers promised to take action against those responsible for his mistreatment. After a brief period, Jesus was given a bath and then transferred to the Divisional Jail, Cester, with authorities citing a non-bailable warrant as the reason for his arrest.

Despite facing numerous rejections, Jesus's well-wishers tirelessly submitted bail petitions on his behalf in the Lower Court. Their efforts bore fruit after three challenging months when Jesus was finally granted bail and released from jail.

Returning to his normal life, Jesus maintained a resilient attitude, acknowledging the obstacles posed by challenging the injustice perpetrated by powerful figures like Harris. He remained steadfast in his determination to seek justice, fully aware of the formidable nature of his adversaries. However, his unwavering hope and confidence in overcoming injustice fuelled his resolve to continue the fight.

Despite the warnings and pressure from some of his neighbours, who belonged to various religious backgrounds, Jesus remained resolute in his pursuit of justice. He asserted that he was not merely battling against a helpless opponent like Harris, but rather challenging an influential figure holding a ministerial post, one who wielded wealth and power. Despite the risks involved, Jesus was determined to expose Harris's wrongdoing and bring an end to his unjust actions. He understood that while Harris may have the ability to harm him or tarnish his reputation, he could never extinguish the truth.

Drawing inspiration from the teachings of figures like Jesus Christ, Lord

Rama, Lord Krishna, and Mahatma Gandhi, Jesus remained steadfast in his belief that righteousness would ultimately prevail. He was unwavering in his conviction that truth would triumph over falsehood, and history would bear witness to this eternal principle.

However, his neighbours, fearing retaliation from Harris, urged him to abandon his pursuit of justice and live peacefully with his two surviving children. They warned him of the dangers of opposing someone as influential as Harris and encouraged him to withdraw the cases he had filed against him. Despite their pleas, Jesus remained steadfast in his commitment to seek justice and bring Harris to account for his actions.

He acknowledged the risks involved in his quest but remained resolute in his commitment to uphold truth and righteousness.

While his neighbours agreed with his ideals in theory, Jesus recognized that their support did not necessarily translate into action in their own lives. He understood that their words were often confined to discussions and lectures, rather than being reflected in their day-to-day actions. However, he remained focused on his mission, determined to confront the injustices perpetrated by Harris.

Despite the perilous nature of his endeavour, Jesus refused to back down. He acknowledged the presence of obstacles along his path but believed that he could overcome them through the strength of his principles. Regardless of the outcome, he remained steadfast in his pursuit of justice, urging his neighbours to wait and witness the eventual triumph of truth.

Continuing his efforts, Jesus reached out to his advocate in the High Court to inquire about the status of his case. He learned that a decision would be reached in one month, further fuelling his resolve to see justice served.

A month had elapsed since the admission of his appeal. Both parties were summoned, and Harris, anticipating the hearing, arrived in Chard a week prior to the scheduled date. He lodged at the Hotel Maharaja accompanied by his bodyguard. From there, he contacted a renowned advocate from the High Court of Chard.

Upon meeting the advocate, Harris greeted him courteously before presenting him with a file. He expressed grave concern, asserting that Jesus had purportedly gone insane. Harris emphasized the seriousness of the matter, framing it as an issue of his honour rather than mere property disputes.

After perusing the documents, the advocate reassured Harris, stating confidently that there were no substantial grounds against him. He assured Harris of his adept handling of such cases, guaranteeing a favourable outcome. To further allay Harris's concerns, the advocate mentioned that the plaintiff's counsel happened to be his younger brother, who could assist in ensuring Harris's silence during the trial, thereby aiding his defence.

Harris, visibly pleased by the prospect of such advantageous circumstances, exclaimed, "Aha! What a stroke of luck! Victory is assured for us!"

The advocate reiterated his assurance, advising Harris to return home and alleviate himself of any worries, assuring him that he would handle the matter competently. He requested only fifty thousand rupees to compensate the plaintiff's counsel for ensuring his silence during the trial. However, he emphasized that Harris need not concern himself with the finances, as their friendship exempted him from any payment.

Reluctant to miss this opportunity, Harris promptly retrieved two bundles of paper currencies from his briefcase and offered them to the advocate. However, the advocate declined one of the bundles, affirming, "I will not accept a single penny for myself, as our friendship transcends monetary concerns. You are my close friend."

Harris retrieved the second bundle of currency and returned it to his briefcase.

The advocate, tucking the remaining bundle into his black coat, expressed his confidence in Harris's victory. He then asked for the details of the case.

Harris, reassured by their friendship, divulged the truth. He admitted to orchestrating a fraudulent sale deed for the land in question, emphasizing that his actions were driven by necessity rather than immorality. He explained that the land held immense value due to its strategic location, adjacent to his own property and along a major road. He acknowledged the assistance of a Registrar, a close associate, in facilitating the deceitful transaction. Despite the fraudulent nature of the deed, Harris boasted of his consistent success in court battles, expressing certainty in his victory with the advocate's assistance.

Furthermore, Harris expressed disdain for Jesus, whom he considered a wayward and vulnerable individual for abandoning his religion and converting to Christianity. Harris ominously threatened his adversary, confident in his ability to wield power and manipulate circumstances to his advantage.

The advocate concurred with Harris, praising his stature and power while disparaging Jesus as directionless and destined for suffering. He remarked that Jesus would likely end up in dire circumstances, perhaps even in hell.

Harris agreed, asserting that not only Jesus but also his children would face similar consequences.

Leaving the conversation behind, both men went their separate ways. Harris, buoyed by the prospect of another legal victory, reflected on the costly nature of his conflict with Jesus. Determined to eliminate him as an obstacle, he summoned his bodyguard to discuss his plans.

"O gallant! It will be best for me if you remove him from my ways."

"Okay, sir! There is no problem. I will remove not only Jesus, rather John, and Joy too."

"You're right. Not only him but rather all. But do all this as soon as possible."

"Don't worry, I will remove them soon and none will know."

Jesus's innocence and virtue shielded him from the malevolent schemes brewing in Harris's mind. Unaware of the impending danger lurking around him and his children, Jesus remained steadfast in his righteousness. Despite his apparent helplessness in the face of worldly evils, Jesus possessed a strength and resilience derived from his unwavering faith and moral integrity. His belief in a higher power, one that transcended the machinations of men like Harris, imbued him with a profound sense of inner strength. In the face of adversity, Jesus remained resolute, drawing strength from his virtues and the divine force that guided his path.

The arrival of the stranger, disguised as a saint, marked the onset of Harris's nefarious plot. Clad in red robes and bearing the semblance of a revered sage, the stranger exuded an aura of sanctity. His attire, from the flowing garments to the iron-made nipper in his hand, lent him an air of authority and mystique. Adorned with the auspicious mark of sandalwood paste on his forehead and sporting a long white beard and moustache, he appeared to be a figure of great reverence.

Jesus, unsuspecting of the danger that lurked beneath the saintly façade, welcomed the stranger into his home. Little did he know that this seemingly pious visitor was but a pawn in Harris's sinister scheme, a harbinger of imminent peril for him and his children.

The stranger's arrival brought a sense of joy and warmth to Jesus, who welcomed him with open arms. He extended his hospitality, inviting the stranger to stay for a week, grateful for the blessing of the saint's presence.

In response, the stranger, masquerading as a senior seer from a nearby monastery, expressed his gratitude for the warm reception. He claimed to be on a divine mission, ordained by God himself, to bestow blessings upon Jesus and his family, citing a supposed encounter with the divine during his worship the previous Sunday.

Deceiving Jesus with false promises, the stranger assured him that within a mere twenty-four hours, he would be relieved of all his burdens and troubles. He went on to promise a bright future for John as a politician and for Joy as a scholar, offering talismans to ensure their success and protection.

Unbeknownst to Jesus, the stranger's benevolent façade concealed a sinister plot, orchestrated by Harris to deceive and manipulate him. With cunning words and false promises, the stranger sought to misguide Jesus and further Harris's malicious intentions. The stranger's guise as a saint proved to be a deceptive prelude to a gruesome tragedy. After bestowing what seemed like blessings upon Jesus and his children, the stranger's true intentions were revealed in a horrifying assault during the night. As the family slept peacefully, they were ambushed by the disguised assailant, who inflicted severe injuries on Jesus and brutally ended the lives of John and Joy.

The morning light unveiled the harrowing aftermath of the attack. Concerned by the absence of John, Joy, and Jesus from their usual activities, the head teacher of St Xavier School, Durban, dispatched a messenger to their home. The grim sight that greeted them – blood seeping from the room and the horrifying discovery of the mutilated bodies – plunged the community into shock and horror.

With John and Joy's lives tragically cut short and Jesus gravely injured, the urgency of the situation prompted their neighbours to swiftly transport Jesus to Edwin Hospital for urgent medical care. Meanwhile, the police launched an investigation, registering a case at the Cester Police Station to pursue justice for the victims.

The saint's malicious deception and violent attack shattered the tranquillity of Jesus and his community, leaving behind a trail of grief and unanswered questions. The head teacher's routine check on student absences took a chilling turn when he discovered the absence of John and Joy, along with Jesus's absence from his gardening duties. Concerned, he dispatched a messenger to investigate their whereabouts.

The media swiftly disseminated news of the tragic incident, with headlines across newspapers capturing the grim reality of the slaughter that claimed the lives of John and Joy while leaving Jesus fighting for survival. The second day following the tragedy saw newspapers prominently featuring the story, framing it as a sensational discovery.

One newspaper's headline read: "Durban Resident Jesus Kills Children, Battles for Life in Hospital." The report portrayed Jesus as a man driven by ambition, alleging that he wielded a sword to end the lives of his own children before attempting to take his own. His condition was described as critical, with little hope for recovery aside from divine intervention. The article painted Jesus as a man without direction, driven by a desire for wealth and a newfound faith in Christianity after abandoning Hinduism. His motives were portrayed as selfish, with accusations of dishonesty and a litigious nature, alluding to his alleged attempt to reclaim land that had long been sold by his father. The narrative even drew parallels between Jesus and the mythological villain Ravana, portraying him as cruel and unscrupulous.

The media's portrayal of the events painted a damning picture of Jesus, shaping public perception and fuelling speculation about the motives behind the gruesome act.

Harris wasted no time in capitalizing on the misleading news coverage surrounding the tragic events. Leveraging the distorted narrative to his advantage, he orchestrated a public gathering where he seized the opportunity to vilify Jesus further. Addressing the crowd, he painted Jesus as a deeply corrupt and morally bankrupt individual, citing the alleged murder of his own sons as evidence of his depravity.

Harris spared no effort in denouncing Jesus, portraying him as a man consumed by greed and deceit, driven by a relentless pursuit of personal gain. He emphasized the alleged attempts by Jesus to reclaim land rightfully purchased by Harris from his father, framing it as a manifestation of his insatiable desire for wealth. With calculated rhetoric, Harris sought to portray himself as a righteous figure, claiming that God had intervened to thwart Jesus's nefarious intentions, thereby vindicating his own actions.

In his impassioned speech, Harris condemned Jesus to eternal damnation, asserting that his place in the afterlife was reserved for hell rather than heaven. He depicted Jesus as a man devoid of virtue, unworthy of redemption or salvation. Harris's rhetoric aimed to instil fear and disdain among the gathered crowd, reinforcing his own moral superiority while demonizing Jesus as a despicable and irredeemable figure.

The media's failure to remain impartial undermined its role as the fourth pillar of democracy. Sensationalized news coverage led common people to believe that Jesus was a cruel man responsible for the death of his children, further reinforcing negative perceptions about his conversion to Christianity. As a result, Harris's popularity surged, with many viewing him as an honest individual unjustly targeted by Jesus's accusations. This biased portrayal fuelled public sentiment against Jesus, painting him as the villain in the narrative and justifying his perceived suffering as a consequence of his actions.

Amidst the prevailing narrative of Jesus's alleged cruelty and wrongdoing, some compared him to Ravana, the mythological figure known for his villainous acts. This comparison further vilified Jesus in the eyes of the public, reinforcing the belief that his conversion to Christianity was the root cause of his misfortune. Some speculated that had he not converted, he would have lived a more pleasant life.

Meanwhile, Jesus lay in the hospital's emergency ward, his condition critical and uncertain. The entire community of Durban anxiously awaited updates on his condition, hoping for any sign of improvement. Despite the uncertainty, people looked to the doctors for reassurance, seeking words of hope and encouragement from those tending to Jesus with their expertise and care.

Despite the dire prognosis delivered by the doctors, the community held onto hope as they watched over Jesus in the hospital. For two weeks, there was little sign of improvement, and despair hung heavy in the air. However, on the eighteenth day, a glimmer of hope emerged as Jesus began to stir and show signs of life. This small indication of progress sparked a flicker of optimism among those gathered around him.

Then, on the thirty-first day of his hospitalization, a significant break-through occurred: Jesus opened his eyes and began to recognize those around him. This moment marked a turning point in his recovery, filling the hearts of those who had been anxiously waiting with renewed hope and joy.

Pardon Them!

Doctors made every effort to save Jesus's life. His neighbours rallied around him, offering unwavering support and adhering to the doctors' every suggestion. Their longing to see him restored to the vibrant member of their community he once was, was palpable.

Thus, he endured a six-month stay in the hospital. Upon his recovery, he returned to the familiarity of his home, unaware of the heartbreaking truth that his children had departed this world. Along the way, he had purchased treats – toffees, biscuits, and sweets – for his beloved children. Upon arriving home, he eagerly called out for John and Joy, unaware that they had slipped into an eternal slumber.

Repeated calls echoed through the silence, but no response came forth. His neighbours, grappling with their own sorrow, found themselves at a loss for words when it came to addressing his loss. Though he questioned them, their tongues were tied, and none could offer solace. It was in this heavy silence that realization dawned upon him.

With a heavy heart, he lowered himself to the ground, placing a trembling hand upon his brow. In the quiet of his home, he began to murmur softly, casting his gaze around as if seeking solace in the memories that lingered in every corner.

Are you John? Are you Joy?
Where are you? Are you in my mortal lap?
You needn't toffees … Biscuits … Sweets?
Will you not run to me? Don't?
Will you not say? Don't?
Why? Why not?
Say! I've come.
After six months.
Only the right hand is gone.

Who I am?
I am Jesus?
What have I had? Only miseries and sorrows?
Arrived in life only to gain justice?

Over injustice?
Only to communicate the divine message?
To bring divine bliss?

Meanwhile, he heard mysterious voices coming from unknown ways:

Don't worry,
I'm wind.
I'm wind.
I'm watching the wind.
Spread over the world.
My angels are at each bidding place.
I watch over sin and virtue –
In water, in the sky, and even in the dust –
I judge bad and good.
Award the divine justice.
None can hide
From my mighty hand –
That I am!

In the meantime, the situation was very distressing. No proper words of consolation came to their tongues. It seemed as though time had momentarily stopped. After some moments, they began to console him. They said not to worry and to try and forget the tragedy. This was the unchangeable law of nature, and tears could not bring them back.

Jesus was usually sitting, his heart turned to stone. He wondered why he was still living. He asked God, "Why am I living here?" There were only tears and sorrows for him. He prayed to God to award heavenly seats to John and Joy and to give him the strength to carry on his struggle for justice against injustice and evil.

He continued to sit there for a moment and uttered some words. After some moments, he prayed to God to pardon those who had committed this act and snatched John and Joy from his lap, because they did not know what they had done.

Restless to see the graves of John and Joy, he went to the village graveyard. James also went along with some other villagers. Seeing their graves, he began to weep bitterly. People tried to console him, but he could not be silent and continued to weep. When all their attempts to pacify him failed, they sat on the ground. Someone began to weep with him. The atmosphere became deeply sorrowful and melancholic.

Anyhow, the situation became normal after some minutes. One by one, they fell silent. They consoled Jesus, saying that this was indeed the holy law of Nature, that each one had to go to their permanent home. This world was a temporary place, and everyone had to leave it one day. No one could ignore this eternal fact. No one could defeat death. No one could gain victory over death. No one could hide from the minute eyes of death, and no one could save themselves from death's cruel hands. Life was full of struggle, and the happiness they felt was false, illusory, and momentary.

People said, "It was indeed a harsh act of God, our Maker. He cast us into this world to remain attached to miseries and sorrows. Attachment was His greatest weapon, entangling us in this world. Life is indeed a market – a vast market of attachment where we are born, grow, and die. Everything and everyone remains here as usual, and we depart with empty hands. This is the essence of life."

Saying all this, they consoled Jesus.

Thus, they gradually returned to normal and went back to their homes. Jesus also became normal after some days. He resumed his daily duties and worked at the school as he had in the past. However, the marks of loss were clearly visible on his face, and sometimes he would become emotional, remembering his sorrow.

In this way, some days passed. He thought about fulfilling the task for which he had been struggling and had faced several tragedies. His neighbours suggested he not pursue justice again. He was also not very interested in proceeding, but his spirit would not allow him to give up. He was seriously contemplating his next step.

In a state of uncertainty about what to do, the spirit of Emily appeared and said to him, "Continue your struggle for the restoration of faith in truth and the abolition of evils. Harris has nothing except sin, which is about to be ended. You are on the right path. Never look back. I am with you. You are not alone. Our children are fine. I look after them."

He witnessed all this mysteriously, so decided to continue his struggle. After a time, he again contacted his counsel to learn the development of the case running in the High Court. He discovered that his appeal had been dismissed just a week earlier.

Upon learning about the case's progress, he became more resolute. He said that he had absolute faith in the Maker and that judgement would be pronounced in his favour. He was confident. Some people did not understand that the wrath of God was revealed from heaven against all ungodliness and the unrighteousness of men who suppressed the truth in unrighteousness. Jesus believed in a faith that should never be gloomy under any circumstances anywhere on this earth.

Despite losing the case, Jesus didn't lose his patience; instead, he became more resolute in seeking justice. He decided to appeal to the Supreme Court against the decision of the High Court, having less than three months to file the appeal. So, he began to prepare.

With only thirty thousand rupees earned, he realized it wasn't sufficient for the expenses involved in the Supreme Court proceedings. Therefore, he borrowed an additional ten thousand rupees from his neighbours. After gathering the necessary funds, he set off for the Supreme Court.

Arriving at the station, he purchased a third-class ticket and boarded a superfast express train. After a two-day journey, he reached his destination. Spending the night in the waiting room of the railway junction, he was determined to proceed with his mission.

The following day, he went to the Supreme Court compound and met with an advocate. He handed over his file containing all documents and narrated his past events in detail, including some informal issues. The advocate carefully reviewed his documents and, upon learning about his past tragedies, became sympathetic and understanding. He listened intently to the mention of Harris.

Understanding the gravity of the situation, the advocate offered his services without any fee. However, Jesus, being conscientious, politely inquired about the advocate's fee, saying, "Sir, please excuse me, sir. What's your fee?"

The advocate explained to Jesus that his usual fee was one lakh rupees, but for a poor sufferer like Jesus, his fee was zero. In reality, the advocate was aligned with Harris's interests, aiming to deceive Jesus, although Jesus was unaware of this fact. Despite Jesus's repeated inquiries about the fee, the advocate insisted that his fee was zero for him. He emphasized this point, making it clear that he was offering his services free of charge, including covering court fees and other expenses. He assured Jesus that he would do everything possible within his knowledge and capacity to help him. The advocate expressed optimism that the case would be resolved within two months, and Jesus would see victory, bringing a smile to his troubled face.

"Sir, I'm very sorry! Take it. I've brought it only for you, not for someone else," Jesus insisted.

"No … Never! I'm not a butcher like others! Go back and pass your life in peace. Don't worry about the case. You must know that now this is not your case, but rather my case. I'll inform you after the disposal of the case," the advocate replied firmly, refusing any payment and asserting his commitment to handling the case on behalf of Jesus.

Seeing such a compassionate man, Jesus felt immense joy. He expressed that he had never encountered such a cooperative, honest, and virtuous individual in his life. He marvelled at the advocate's integrity and goodness, noting that there was no distinction between his name and his actions. Wherever there was mercy, the advocate could be found, demonstrating rare goodness and greatness.

However, the advocate remained humble, acknowledging that he was merely fulfilling his duty as a servant of the poor and helpless. He emphasized that service was his purpose in life, instilled in him by his upbringing.

Despite the advocate's noble intentions, Jesus was unaware of the counsel's true motives, as his gentlemanly demeanour obscured any ulterior motives. Jesus maintained his belief in justice and hoped for a positive outcome.

Before departing, Jesus thanked the advocate for his kindness and explained that he was returning to Durban. He insisted that the advocate accept the forty thousand rupees he had brought solely for him, hoping it would alleviate some of his burdens.

Reluctantly, the advocate accepted the money with gratitude and urged Jesus to return home. Jesus bid farewell, saluting the advocate, and departed for his home, carrying with him a mixture of gratitude and hope for the future.

The counsel for Jesus diligently followed through on his promises. He prepared and filed the draft of the case as planned. Within a week, a notice was served to Harris. Upon receiving the notice, Harris's reaction was fierce and alarming.

Witnesses described his face at that moment as resembling an object of fire. His cheeks flushed red, blood trickled from his mouth, and his eyes blazed with anger. He erupted in a torrent of vulgar abuse directed at Jesus and all Christians. In his fury, he threw the dish of food he was eating and smashed his mobile phone against the television screen, vowing to deal with Jesus and the Christians before attending to anything else.

A witness who was present when the notice was served recounted the scene, describing Harris as extremely angry and intent on causing harm to Jesus if he encountered him. He berated his bodyguard, questioning why he had allowed Jesus to remain alive until now. Harris also vented his frustration to his family members, lamenting that despite amassing millions through unfair means for their benefit, they had not taken care of any issues, leaving him to deal with all matters alone. His agitation was evident as he continued to erupt in a torrent of furious outbursts.

Harris expressed his frustration, emphasizing that he had amassed millions for the family, not just for himself. Yet, despite his efforts, they had done nothing, leaving him to handle everything alone, which constantly disturbed him. He acknowledged that they would inherit his wealth but not the sins he had committed throughout his life. While he ensured their enjoyment of his earnings, he viewed this issue as a matter of his honour and millions, which he refused to let slip from his grasp. However, he declared that after resolving this case, he would no longer handle any matters for them. It was their responsibility to handle any issues beneficial to the family from then on.

Realizing that Jesus had reached the apex court, Harris recognized the gravity of the situation. He contemplated the power he wielded and the wealth he had amassed to fight cases against Jesus. Harris vowed that after the final decision on the case, he would reveal Jesus's true identity and his own. He believed that Jesus perceived himself as a prophet but was ignorant of the harsh realities of the world. Harris doubted whether anyone ever truly received justice in this world, understanding this fact completely.

Harris's thoughts consumed him, and he lost his temper as the weight of his predicament and the problems facing his family weighed heavily on him.

Harris, consumed by frustration, displayed a clear sense of apathy. Despite his agitation, he was determined to secure victory in the apex court at any cost, viewing it as a matter of his honour. To bolster his chances of success, he initiated efforts and summoned a reputed advocate to his residence for a discussion.

During their meeting, Harris implored the advocate to take his case file seriously, emphasizing the importance of the matter to his honour. He claimed that Jesus was defaming him by frequently filing cases against him, thereby tarnishing his reputation and popularity. Harris urgently requested the advocate's assistance in this critical situation, expressing his willingness to reward him with a nomination to the Upper House of Parliament if he could help him.

The advocate listened attentively to Harris's plea, understanding the gravity of the situation. "Don't worry, this is like a game for me, I will deal with it accordingly. I understand your current situation, and my sympathy is entirely for you."

Having reassured Harris in a polite and reassuring manner, advising him not to worry, he reminded Harris that if he felt anxious, he could consider the plight of a common man and find solace in the fact that everything would eventually fall into place. The advocate pledged his unwavering support, promising to exhaust every possible avenue to ensure Harris's victory.

Feeling relieved after his discussion with the counsel, Harris breathed a sigh of relief. He believed that with the advocate's help, his problems would soon be resolved. He found peace and rested, anticipating a favourable outcome and his victory in the apex court.

However, when the first day of the hearing arrived, neither the defence nor the prosecution counsels were present in court. As a result, the hearing was postponed to the following Monday. This scenario repeated over the subsequent dozen hearing dates, with both counsels continuously absent, leading to repeated adjournments by the judge.

The Trial by God

Time takes its toll on all, and it began to take its toll on Harris and others who were culpable in the matters concerning Jesus. The citizens of Durban were thoroughly discontented with the constabulary for their failure to apprehend the wrongdoers. Consequently, they exerted mounting pressure on law enforcement to swiftly and decisively act in arresting those at fault. However, despite their efforts, the police remained inert, and no arrests were made. This only fuelled further dissatisfaction. Subsequently, a strike was called within the city as a manifestation of the increasing pressure. The outcome revealed the glaring inertia of the police force to the public. Following the strike, the government also began to show interest in the case, prompting an official directive for the police to take appropriate action against the guilty parties.

The daily newspapers frequently covered news concerning the Jesus matter, prompting a surge in police activity. Law enforcement faced the daunting task of apprehending the individuals involved, which proved to be no mean feat. Consequently, police officers became highly proactive, conducting extensive visits to various locations in pursuit of the culprits. On the same day, two individuals participating in a religious service at a temple in a remote village were taken into custody. Following their arrest, the police announced that both suspects in the Jesus case had been apprehended.

However, some individuals began to assert that the arrested individuals were entirely innocent, claiming they had no knowledge of the matter whatsoever.

With public criticism mounting against them, the police found themselves with no recourse but to apprehend the guilty parties. The following day, officers proceeded to another village where they arrested four individuals who were tending to their fields. Subsequently, they were escorted to the Cester Police Station. Members of the media were summoned to the station, where it was announced that the detainees were implicated in the murder of Jesus's children. However, the accused vehemently denied any involvement, asserting their innocence and claiming ignorance regarding Jesus and the reason for their arrest. They maintained that they had been occupied with their agricultural duties when the police arrived to take them into custody. The subsequent day, newspapers reported the arrests of the four individuals, detailing their incarceration, yet highlighting their persistent denial of culpability.

Conversely, the police maintained that the arrested individuals were solely responsible for the matters concerning Jesus. However, the populace remained unconvinced of their involvement in Jesus's affairs. Consequently, a procession was organized to denounce their arrest in front of the Superintendent of Police. In response, the Superintendent of Police issued a directive for the apprehension of all culpable individuals involved in both James's and Jesus's cases within twenty-four hours. The detained individuals remained in police custody pending further investigation into the cases.

The following morning, police officers descended upon the banks of the Toss River, where they apprehended seven individuals who were bathing as part of a festival celebration. Subsequently, they were escorted to the police station and subjected to severe beatings by the officers. Under duress, they confessed to their alleged transgressions.

The police then summoned the media to report on the incident. They instructed reporters to document their account, claiming that all the guilty parties had been bathing together in the Toss River. They asserted that acting on intelligence, they swiftly moved to the location and arrested all seven suspects simultaneously. They encouraged journalists to inquire further if there were any doubts or confusion surrounding the matter.

The arrested individuals, under the threat of further violence, reluctantly admitted to their supposed crimes with a single word, "yes." They succumbed to the pressure, believing that refusal would only result in more beatings. Thus, they falsely confessed to their alleged offenses. The truth of the matter remained obscured, unbeknownst to all at the time.

The subsequent day, news of their arrest proliferated across the pages of numerous newspapers, leading many to believe that the suspects had indeed been apprehended. Some members of the public even speculated that the police had targeted innocent individuals as a diversionary tactic to deflect attention from the true perpetrators.

Meanwhile, a new development emerged in the case. The government had clandestinely commissioned a special committee within the Criminal Investigation Department to probe all matters related to Jesus. This committee operated covertly, its activities shielded from the knowledge of the general populace. Despite months passing, the committee had yet to submit its report, leaving the investigation shrouded in mystery.

A pivotal moment occurred in Jesus's case with the submission of the committee's report and the filing of a petition before the special court of the apex court. The truth was finally unveiled. According to the report, both officers and medical professionals bore responsibility for Jesus's ordeal, as outlined in the detailed findings. It exposed the individuals involved in the removal of Jesus's eye and kidney, identified those who engaged in the illicit trade of his organs, revealed the pricing involved, exposed the perpetrators of Jesus's children's murders, shed light on those who aided Harris in his wrongdoing, and elucidated the role of law enforcement.

The comprehensive report laid bare all hidden facts, presenting them transparently before the public eye. This revelation precipitated a significant shift in the situation surrounding the case.

- "It emerged that the recorded sale deed, which conferred ownership to Harris in the Registrar's office, was fraudulent. Harris bore primary responsibility for all the misfortunes inflicted upon Jesus. Harris stood as the principal defendant in the case alongside the former Registrar, the Circle Officer, the Land Reforms Deputy Commissioner, the Chief Commission-er, the District Judge, the Superintendent of Police, the District Magistrate, and two named physicians at the time …"

- "Huda was additionally charged with the homicides of Jesus's two children. The former physician had extracted Jesus's kidney and sold it to a Russian citizen for twenty lakh rupees. Another doctor had removed Jesus's left eye and sold it to an American citizen for ten lakh rupees."

- "Harris orchestrated the fabrication of a fraudulent sale deed in his favour, with assistance from the then Registrar. Exploiting illegal and unethical advantages, the District Judge ruled in favour of Harris. Similarly, the Circle Officer rendered a decision in favour of Harris for personal gain. The Lower Court Judge sided with Harris solely to reap unlawful benefits. When Jesus persisted in seeking justice, Harris orchestrated the murders of John and Joy by Huda, who posed as a saint. In doing so, Harris also attempted to besmirch the sacred reputation of saints."

- Harris had conspired to have Jesus murdered by Huda, but fate intervened, sparing Jesus with only the loss of his right hand. The then Superintendent of Police was also implicated in the aforementioned murders, ordering the Police Inspector to cease the investigation. A nameless case was registered merely to fulfil formalities."

• "Thus, they too bore responsibility for the misfortunes inflicted upon Jesus. Jesus, indeed, was entirely innocent. Being Jesus – Jesus Smith – his life could not be claimed by a notorious criminal like Huda, and he embarked on a new chapter in his life."

• "The Edwin Hospital in Malabar played a pivotal role in saving his life by providing six months of free treatment. Harris, albeit indirectly, bore primary responsibility for the deaths of Emily, Levi, and Luke. These revelations, brought to light by the secret committee, served as a wake-up call for the public."

The Investigation Committee submitted a sixty-seven-page report, supported by four hundred pages of records and statements from twenty-nine witnesses. The Judge admitted the case to the committee and summoned all the accused and witnesses mentioned. People were astonished by this turn of events, with many who had previously supported Harris now shifting their allegiance to Jesus.

The following day, numerous newspapers ran headlines under "the Trial of God." This report and petition sparked an unexpected turn of events, prompting discussions nationwide. People remarked on the resilience of the law, the impartiality of the police, and the transient nature of taking matters into one's own hands. The revelation bolstered public faith in the judiciary and executive branches, becoming a topic of widespread discourse across India.

Responding to the significance of the case, the Chief Justice of the Supreme Court ordered a special court to consolidate and hear all related cases, including Jesus's old case. The court was directed to hold regular hearings, which would be recorded by video camera. Additionally, a special bench of five judges was appointed, provided with high-grade security due to the sensitivity of the cases involving a Central Government minister, frequently highlighted by the media.

The media remained deeply engaged in covering the daily developments of the case, keeping the public well-informed and intrigued by the issues surrounding Jesus and Harris.

Meanwhile, as a fresh case was filed against Harris, opposition members of parliament intensified pressure on the government to remove him from the cabinet. However, the government staunchly defended Harris, stating that he would not resign until the case reached a conclusion and refuting the charges against him as false. Despite mounting calls for his resignation, Harris remained adamant about retaining his position in the cabinet.

He defiantly stated, "The allegations brought forth by the Criminal Investigation Department are nothing but attempts to tarnish my reputation and undermine my popularity, all aimed at removing me from the cabinet and halting my ongoing efforts for the welfare of the impoverished and vulnerable. I categorically refuse to resign from my post until the case is resolved, and I remain steadfast in my commitment to advocating for the rights of the underprivileged."

The strategy to secure victory in the Supreme Court, with the assistance of Harris's familiar counsel, faltered with the initiation of a new case against Harris and his associates. The tide of events seemed to be swiftly turning in favour of Jesus, prompting some to interpret it as a victory for Truth or God.

Despite mounting pressure from opposition parties, Harris remained steadfast in his refusal to resign. Consequently, the President, acting upon the recommendation of the Prime Minister, dismissed him from the cabinet. Within a week, all the accused, except Harris, were arrested. Harris, however, obtained anticipatory bail, enabling him to avoid incarceration.

Both parties were summoned, and the hearing commenced without interruption. The proceedings took place on a Friday, marking the inaugural session of the special court convened for this purpose. All judges of the special bench were in attendance. However, the defence counsel was conspicuously absent, prompting the postponement of the hearing until the following day.

On Saturday, the second day of the hearing, the judges were present, yet the defence counsel failed to appear once more. Consequently, the hearing was adjourned once again, this time until the next working day.

On Monday, the defence counsel arrived but was significantly delayed, resulting in another adjournment of the court until the following day. However, the following day, the counsel was once again absent. The defence counsel persisted in obstructing the trial proceedings for fifteen days, citing medical reasons.

Throughout the trial, Harris spared no effort to evade the grasp of the law, which some believed to be as powerful as the hands of time and God. Initially, he attempted to summon the honourable judges to his residence, but none of them acceded to his request. Undeterred, he persistently called them seeking their assistance, only to be met with firm refusals to engage with him. Despite his efforts, the judges remained unresponsive.

Subsequently, Harris resorted to visiting their homes, yet he was rebuffed, denied even a single cup of tea. His last resort was reaching out to their relatives, but this endeavour also proved fruitless as they refrained from meeting him until the case was resolved. Furthermore, the judges postponed participating in any public events or leaving their residences, effectively thwarting all of Harris's attempts to influence them.

Surrounded on all sides and with his private bodyguard and co-accused already incarcerated, Harris found himself losing his composure. His hopes of using his wealth and influence for protection had been dashed, leaving him frustrated and agitated.

The report deeply unsettled Harris, leading him to denounce the judges as corrupt and unworthy of their titles. He likened them to dogs, accusing them of refusing to meet even a Member of Parliament – a member of the New Socialist Party and a former Law Minister. In his frustration, he questioned their sanity, emphasizing the power they wielded to send individuals to ruin. Harris speculated on their future after retirement, suggesting they may face obscurity or confinement. His remarks reflected his growing disillusionment and resentment towards the judicial system. Harris's frustration boiled over, and he launched into a scathing tirade, declaring that the judges were no better than dogs that merely barked within the confines of their homes. He threatened to crush them with his bare fists, confident that they wouldn't even whimper in response. Harris ominously reminded them of the power he wielded as a former Law Minister, insinuating that he had the capability to ruin each of them without hesitation. His warning was clear and uncompromising.

Harris's frustration reached such heights that he appeared unhinged at times, resembling a madman. His nerves were frayed, leading to instances where he lashed out with abusive language even towards his own family members. Despite their efforts to calm him and encourage patience, reminding him of his influence and the expected outcome of the trial in his favour due to his stature, Harris remained unable to regain his composure. His frequent outbursts of abuse underscored his deep-seated agitation and anxiety.

Harris's discontent with his family members reached its peak. He lamented that despite all his efforts to elevate the family's honour and stature, he alone bore the burden of managing everything. In his anger, he expressed his belief that he stood unrivalled within his dynasty, having single-handedly propelled his family to its current status. However, despite his sacrifices, he felt unappreciated and burdened by the responsibilities he bore alone.

The constant stream of court notices added to his distress, robbing him of the peace and tranquillity he once enjoyed. He lamented that even the loyalty of those around him seemed to have waned, as no one responded to his calls anymore. This sense of isolation and abandonment fuelled his frustration further. Nevertheless, he vowed to restore order, asserting his influence as a former minister. Harris's words and actions reflected the depths of his frustration and disillusionment.

It's evident that Harris's frustration and verbal abuse had little impact on those around him, including his family members and the judges presiding over his case, who continued with the hearings unperturbed. As he approached the consequences of his actions, Harris found himself in a state he never anticipated. Despite his previous confidence in his immunity from harm, he now realized he was at the mercy of time, waiting and enduring his fate.

Facing this realization, Harris underwent a significant transformation. He turned to religious practices, spending hours in worship, fasting for the expiation of his sins, and visiting various temples. He made promises to donate gold and money to temples, seeking solace and redemption. At times, he felt a sense of connection with the divine, believing that his prayers were heard and that he was promised protection from harm. This shift in behaviour reflected his desperate attempt to find peace and assurance in the face of impending judgment.

For and Against

Now the situation of Harris was beyond imagination. The events unfolding were entirely unforeseen, demonstrating how a man can be ensnared after committing numerous wrongdoings. He made strenuous efforts to contact the judges and exert his influence, but despite all his attempts, no one would meet him.

Amidst this, the trial in the special court commenced. He found himself firmly in the grip of time, with no options left to evade the trial. Despite his desperate efforts to escape the scrutiny of the law, all his attempts were in vain.

When the hearing began, the prosecution counsel addressed the bench, arguing that Harris, the principal accused in the case, was the root cause of all the crimes committed.

- He asserted that Harris had orchestrated the murders of Jesus's children and had attempted to murder Jesus himself. The actions were executed by Huda, Harris's private bodyguard.
- Harris, a Member of Parliament and the wealthiest man in Worcester, had abused his position and wealth. He had fabricated a bogus sale deed to misappropriate the small and sole piece of land belonging to a poor and helpless man like Jesus, showcasing his immoral and illegal desires. Consequently, Harris was deemed guilty of all the crimes that had brought tragedy to Jesus's life.
- The prosecution counsel urged the court to impose the severest punishment on Harris and Huda under various sections of the law.
- Additionally, the former Registrar, Circle Officer, Land Reforms Deputy Commissioner, Chief Commissioner, District Judge, Superintendent of Police, and District Magistrate had all aided Harris in fulfilling his illegal ambitions, driven by the prospect of illegal gains. The former doctor had removed Jesus's right kidney and sold it to a Russian citizen for twenty lakh rupees, while another doctor had removed Jesus's left eye and sold it to an American citizen for ten lakh rupees.
- Harris, a public representative, had committed numerous crimes despite

his position of responsibility, thereby exacerbating the severity of his actions.

- Harris and the other accused had engaged a dozen defence counsels who presented their arguments to the bench. They emphasised that Harris, the primary accused, was a responsible individual – a Member of Parliament, a former Law Minister, and a senior leader of the New Socialist Party. Given his status, it was inconceivable that he could have committed such crimes. They described Harris as an honest man, always dedicated to serving the poor and the suffering.

The defence highlighted Harris's significant contributions, noting that he was the first Law Minister in the country's history to propose a landmark resolution in Parliament aimed at reforming outdated laws for the benefit of the poor and helpless. This, they argued, demonstrated his integrity and commitment to public service, making the charges against him implausible.

- The charges against Harris were politically motivated, designed by other leaders to tarnish his reputation and diminish his popularity. They claimed there was no factual basis for the case and that the accusations were baseless.
- Regarding Huda, the second chief accused, the defence maintained his innocence, asserting he had no involvement in the murders. They pointed out that Jesus's children had been killed by a saint, and at the time of the murders, Huda was in the capital, not in Worcester. They described Huda as a gentle and polite individual who had never harmed even a mosquito, making the allegations against him implausible and the investigation committee's charges unauthentic.
- The integrity of the Superintendent of Police. He had received recognition for gallantry. Any doubts about his involvement in the murders were unfounded, given his commendable service record. All charges against him were false and baseless.
- They Land Reforms Deputy Commissioner was an honest officer who had been recognised for his integrity and service. As such, he could never act against government laws. The decision he delivered, which stated that the land was in Harris's possession and not Jesus's, was entirely lawful and correct. Therefore, the charges against him were clearly unfounded, and implored the judges to dismiss them.
- Similarly, the District Judge was portrayed as a virtuous and honest man dedicated to true service. His decisions were based on his extensive legal

knowledge and understanding, asserting that he would never act against the law. Consequently, the charges against him were also baseless and illusory.

- The Registrar was a well-known government officer celebrated for his honesty and truthfulness. The sale deed registered in his office was legitimate, bearing the thumb impression of Jesus's father. Jesus's current attempt to claim Harris's land was driven by greed and a lack of moral direction, rendered the charges against the Registrar unauthentic and baseless.

- The Chief Commissioner was portrayed as an honest government officer, devoted to upholding the law above all else. He had adhered strictly to legal principles and had dismissed Jesus's appeal to prevent the misappropriation of land, underscoring his commitment to justice. Thus, the charges against him were entirely unfounded and the judges were implored to dismiss all charges against these individuals.

- The doctors were dedicated professionals committed to their oaths to serve patients with the utmost medical knowledge and awareness. The first doctor had saved Jesus's life when he was on his deathbed, with no one else to help him. Jesus had ungratefully forgotten the doctor's services and had become a victim of malice and prejudice.

- Regarding the second doctor, his duty and responsibility as a government hospital doctor was commendable. They found it unimaginable that he had taken Jesus's left eye, asserting that Jesus had been unconscious and severely injured when the police brought him to the hospital. The doctor had been the sole individual able to save Jesus's life at that critical moment. By saving Jesus, the doctor had demonstrated virtue, not committed a crime. The charges against this honest doctor were the result of misperception and prejudice.

After more than two months of daily hearings, the special court convicted all the accused. The public, elated by the court's findings, eagerly anticipated severe punishments for the guilty parties.

The court presented its findings after careful and thorough legal consideration of all the evidence presented by the plaintiffs, defendants, and witnesses. It concluded that Harris was the primary instigator of all the crimes in the case. He initiated the fabrication of a bogus sale deed to unlawfully seize Jesus's paternal land, with the assistance of other implicated officers. When Jesus sought justice through legal means, Harris resorted to further illegal, immoral, antisocial, and inhumane actions to secure victory over Jesus, truth, and justice. In doing so, he disregarded his position of responsibility.

Regarding the doctors involved, one had deceitfully removed Jesus's right kidney under the guise of a major abdominal operation and sold it to a Russian citizen for twenty lakh rupees – an egregious crime for which the court convicted him.

Similarly, another doctor had extracted Jesus's left eye and sold it to an American citizen for ten lakh rupees, leading to his conviction by the court.

After the court rendered its verdict of conviction against all the accused, the proceedings were adjourned until the following day. This represented Jesus's final opportunity for legal recourse, and he remained resolute in his pursuit of justice. Confident in his role as a true servant of God, Jesus reflected on his unwavering commitment despite facing adversity. He often contemplated the divine intervention in his situation.

On the subsequent day, Jesus prepared himself for his court appearance, fully aware of the gravity of the situation. Despite the circumstances, he remained ensconced in a state of hopeful anticipation, clinging to the possibility of a favourable outcome.

As he sat on the ground, his hand resting on his head, Jesus engaged in a soliloquy. Despite his purity and unwavering faith, he found himself ensnared in a profound dilemma. The world, once a place of solace, now felt like a thorn in his side. He pondered the apparent injustice of his plight, wondering why, despite his innocence, he had endured so much suffering. It seemed as though even God had ordained his tribulations, leading some to question the fairness of divine will.

Despite his efforts to seek legal redress, Jesus found himself met with further injustice at the hands of the very judges entrusted with upholding the law. From the lower courts to the highest echelons of the judiciary, he encountered only disappointment and injustice. His losses extended beyond the courtroom, as society's injustices swallowed his wife and two minor children into the abyss of poverty, while his other children succumbed to the influence of evil forces. The doctors, sworn to serve humanity, had callously taken his left eye and right kidney, leaving him bereft of hope and everything he held dear.

In that fleeting moment of doubt, Jesus momentarily wavered in his faith, a natural response to the immense trials he faced. However, beneath this momentary lapse lay an unwavering trust in God, an unshakeable foundation of his being.

Alone with his thoughts, Jesus pondered his next steps, lost in the labyrinth of his own mind. Amidst this contemplation, a miraculous occurrence unfolded before him.

Suddenly, a figure cloaked in saintly attire materialized before his eyes, emanating an aura of divine grace.

The appearance of this celestial being left Jesus in awe, rendering him speechless in the presence of such divine majesty. Though no words escaped his lips, his heart and mind were filled with wonder at the sight before him.

Addressing Jesus with solemn authority, the stranger acknowledged the illusionary nature of his current reality, prompting Jesus to prepare himself for a deeper understanding. This enigmatic encounter hinted at profound revelations to come, urging Jesus to be steadfast in readiness for the journey ahead.

He spoke to Jesus, his words carrying an air of divine wisdom, "Reflect on your actions and contributions to the world. Consider what you have bestowed upon it. But remember, it is God who has orchestrated all, bestowed all, and reclaimed all. Only He holds the power to enact such deeds. Who created the world and all within it? Who breathed life into your being? Who bestowed upon you the blessing of four children? It is God who has bestowed these gifts upon you, orchestrating every facet of your existence. There exists a mysterious purpose behind all occurrences, beyond your comprehension. It is not your right nor your duty to grasp the intricacies of divine reasoning. Understand this fundamental truth: the righteous are invariably rewarded, while the wicked face their due punishment."

Jesus absorbed the words of the celestial visitor with serene acceptance, finding solace in their profound wisdom. With a sense of contentment, he replied, "Truly, I am unworthy to respond to such divine truths. I shall refrain from uttering another word."

In the presence of truth's illumination, Jesus found himself enveloped in a sense of peace. The celestial visitor assured him that God would restore his fortunes in due time, urging him to await the appointed hour.

With a final decree, the stranger emphasized the unrivalled supremacy of God's divine light, assuring Jesus that justice would prevail. The promise of retribution for the wicked and abundant blessings for the righteous filled Jesus with hope and assurance.

As suddenly as he had appeared, the celestial visitor vanished, leaving behind a profound sense of wonder and awe. Truly, it was a miracle beyond comprehension.

On the other side, one night, an unusual occurrence befell Harris as he lay in bed, his wife sleeping beside him. In a moment of intimacy, he kissed her and sought solace in the comfort of their union amidst his troubles. Yet, to his shock, he discovered that he was embracing not his wife, but a ghastly apparition, its skeletal form devoid of flesh and muscle. It appeared to be a lifeless statue.

The sight filled Harris with terror, causing him to lose consciousness for a brief moment. Upon regaining his senses, he found himself alone in the room, the door securely locked from within, with no sign of anyone else present.

This eerie encounter left Harris bewildered and shaken, pondering the inexplicable events that had transpired in the dead of night.

During those tumultuous days, Harris's mental state deteriorated to a dire condition. He became increasingly withdrawn, haunted by visions of Emily and her four deceased children, their spectral forms manifesting everywhere he turned. Oscillating between moments of terror and despair, he would often cry out in fear at the sight of these apparitions, feeling utterly disconnected from reality.

In his delirium, Harris's thoughts became consumed by notions of litigation and criminality. He would mutter names of notorious criminals, convinced of his own invincibility and their unwavering allegiance to him. He harboured delusions of wielding absolute power, believing himself beyond the reach of any opposition.

One fateful day, as he sat down to eat, he relished the flavours of his meal until he was suddenly confronted with a mouthful of salt. The shock of this discovery induced vomiting, leaving him feeling as though he were ensnared in the grasp of malevolent spirits. In his disoriented state, he perceived a ghastly sight: a lifeless figure lay upon his bed, a serpent coiled around its neck, a grim omen of impending doom.

The following day brought yet another inexplicable occurrence into Harris's life. Seated in his elegantly decorated dining room, he began to partake of his meal. However, to his astonishment, the food before him inexplicably transformed into sand, leaving him with a mouthful of grit. The sudden transformation bewildered all present, and Harris himself felt besieged by supernatural forces. He couldn't shake the feeling that the vengeful spirits of Emily and her children were exacting their revenge upon him, leaving him in a state of shock and despair. This bizarre phenomenon became a recurring occurrence, robbing Harris of any semblance of peace for the remainder of his days.

On another occasion, as Harris sat down to drink milk alongside his wife and children, he was met with yet another startling revelation. While his family's milk remained unchanged, Harris's own portion inexplicably turned into blood, filling his mouth with its coppery taste. This unsettling experience only served to compound Harris's frustration and bewilderment, further cementing his belief that he was the target of otherworldly torment.

Indeed, Harris found himself besieged by a series of inexplicable and unsettling events. Whether it was the sight of a jackal accompanying him, or the unsettling presence of a serpent in his bed, each occurrence left him shaken to the core. Nightmares plagued his sleep, with cries of "serpent … serpent" echoing through the darkness. Even during seemingly mundane activities like bathing, he found himself confronted with the surreal sensation of blood instead of water.

These experiences took a toll on Harris, leaving him deeply troubled and agitated. At times, he confided in his family, expressing a sense of impending doom and remorse for his past actions against Jesus. In moments of desperation, he pleaded for forgiveness from a higher power. However, he failed to grasp the immutable truth that every action carries consequences, and no one can escape the repercussions of their deeds.

The tables had turned dramatically. Once haunted by the fear of ghosts himself, Jesus now found himself in a position of relative peace, while Harris grappled with his own terrifying encounters. The spectre of ghosts seemed to haunt every corner of his home, driving him to cry out in fear. His family, deeply troubled by his deteriorating mental state, sought every avenue for his treatment, but their efforts proved futile.

In a desperate attempt to find relief, they turned to a renowned sorcerer for help. However, instead of receiving aid, the sorcerer was met with hostility and violence from Harris, who lashed out in a fit of rage. As the sorcerer fled from the scene, he lamented the formidable presence of the ghost that seemed to possess Harris's home, describing it as an entity of unparalleled dread.

Caught in the grip of fear and turmoil, Harris's plight seemed to mirror the ghostly apparitions that tormented him, leaving his family at a loss for how to bring an end to their haunting ordeal.

Revelation

The sweltering heat of the June day was unbearable, breaking records that spanned over a century. Trees stood bare, their leaves seemingly shed in lament for water that seemed scarce. Naked stems reached out into the dry air, while the parched earth lay strewn with fallen leaves, carried away by the relentless gusts of the west wind.

Seeds lay dormant, awaiting the life-giving rains of the impending monsoon, as peasants took respite from their toil, their granaries filled with the golden yield of the fields. The scorching rays of the sun had burnt the very grass of the earth, rendering its surface hot enough to bake bread.

People, weary from the relentless summer heat, cast hopeful gazes toward the sky, longing for the arrival of the monsoon clouds to bring relief to the parched land.

In the stifling heat of the courtroom, the accused stood in the dock, their fate hanging in the balance. Unlike the peasants eagerly awaiting the monsoon, they awaited a legal verdict that would determine their future.

Their once-active demeanour had been replaced by a sombre stillness, as if they already knew the outcome of the impending decision. Their bodies seemed as dry and withered as the stems of summer, their faces bearing the nakedness of the earth's surface in this scorching season. Lost in thought, they wore worn but meticulously clean garments, eschewing the fashionably new cuts favoured by the upper-middle-class society.

Conversation amongst them was sparse, their focus solely on the imminent judgment that would seal their fate. Silence enveloped them, their demeanour akin to that of individuals facing the solemnity of a deceased cow mother lying before them. Despite Jesus's gaze upon them, it was not one of mockery, but rather a silent reflection on the days when they had perpetrated their wrongs and sought to extinguish his life.

The accused box exuded an aura of the crimes that had been perpetrated within it. It felt as though, with each passing day, some unseen shift was occurring in the very fabric of the earth's rotation. To some observers, it seemed as though the floor of the accused box itself was descending, threatening to consume those who stood upon it. Whether this phenomenon was real or merely a trick of perception remained a matter of debate among the common folk, although there were those who claimed to have witnessed it firsthand.

The faces of the accused were the subject of intense discussion, akin to how hunters might dissect their prey after a successful hunt. Yet, the accused themselves appeared passive, while Jesus radiated an aura of activity. The court, too, was alive with purpose, actively working to determine the fate of those in the accused box and deliver the consequences of their actions.

The anticipation for the long-awaited decision in this case was palpable, as it stood out as one of the rarest among rare cases. Never before had the court seen such a clash between an influential figure like Harris and a humble, helpless man like Jesus. This unique circumstance sparked discussions across all corners of society, from crossroads to restaurants, offices to houses, and hotels to pathways.

For many, this case symbolized more than just a legal proceeding; it was seen as a pivotal moment that could potentially restore faith in the court's ability to deliver justice for the poor against the powerful. It was viewed as a battle not just between individuals, but between broader concepts of justice and injustice, virtue and sin, goodness and evil. The outcome of this case was expected to have far-reaching implications, resonating deeply with the collective conscience of society.

The scene outside the courtroom was tense, with an old man anxiously awaiting the outcome of the trial. He expressed his belief that if justice were served to Jesus, it would restore the common people's faith in the judiciary. His gaze pierced through the accused as if they were caged tigers in a zoo. The accused, in turn, glared back at the crowd, particularly focusing their ire on the old man who seemed to be scrutinizing them intently.

The old man didn't hesitate to point out the accused, drawing attention to their alleged crimes – removing Jesus's eye, taking his kidney, and being responsible for the death of his children. The accused seethed with anger, their frustration evident, but they remained confined to the accused box, unable to retaliate against the accusations hurled their way. It was a moment of intense anticipation as everyone awaited the judgment to be handed down by the bench of judges.

Despite discussions about the compelling evidence against Harris and the other accused, many people still held doubts about Jesus's chances of winning the case. Harris's influence and his past position as a government minister led them to believe that the outcome might not favour Jesus. All eyes were on the impending judgment, eagerly awaiting its pronouncement.

Meanwhile, Jesus stood quietly in a corner, contemplating his future. He seemed neither elated nor despondent, almost indifferent to the buzzing mosquitoes that continued to bite him. Lost in his thoughts, he appeared to have a sense of acceptance about what lay ahead – be it triumph or defeat. Some speculated that he drew strength from a spiritual source, enabling him to confront the injustice perpetrated by Harris and his cohorts.

In the quiet moments of contemplation, Jesus found solace in the verses of Thomas Hardy's "To The Moon," his murmurs carrying the weight of Hardy's poignant words:

> *What have you looked at, moon,*
> *In your prime,*
> *Now long past your prime?*
>
> *O, I have looked at, often looked at*
> *Sweet, sublime,*
> *Sore things, shudderful, night and noon*
> *In my time.*

The lines echoed through his mind, offering him a semblance of comfort and understanding amidst the turmoil of his circumstances.

As the court filled with eager spectators, the atmosphere crackled with anticipation. The judges presided over the scene from their seats, flanked by the diligent clerk who aided them in their proceedings. Meanwhile, the vigilant police officers maintained a watchful eye over the crowd, employing modern surveillance techniques to ensure order and security. Among the attendees were supporters of Harris, hopeful for a verdict in their favour, their presence adding to the charged atmosphere within the courtroom.

Harris stood with a sombre demeanour, his gaze fixed upon the ground. His once-proud stature now diminished, his form appearing gaunt and frail, with bones protruding visibly. Despite a guilty smile gracing his lips, there was an air of humility about him, stripped of the pomp and arrogance he once possessed. Lost in contemplation, he pondered his past actions and the uncertain future ahead. At times, he closed his eyes in silent prayer, though no words escaped his lips, no outward signs of agitation or fury displayed. He appeared almost gentlemanly, the veneer of influence and power faded, replaced by unmistakable traces of despair etched upon his countenance.

In the meantime, the spirits of Emily and her children appeared before Harris.

As Harris beheld the haunting figures of Emily and her children, a wave of intense emotions coursed through him. His heart raced, and a shiver ran down his spine as he experienced a chilling thrill in the presence of these spectral beings. The sheer disbelief and terror of encountering the apparitions filled him with an unsettling excitement, sending a rush of adrenaline coursing through his veins. In that moment, Harris found himself caught between fascination and fear, unable to tear his gaze away from the ghostly apparitions before him.

As the spectres hovered before him, Harris's voice trembled with fear and desperation. "Ghosts ... ghosts ... save me ..." he uttered, his words choked with terror. "One ... two ... three ... four ... five ... Why have you all come here? Will you kill me? You are stretching my soul. Oh ... you are warning me, showing fingers ... knives in your hands ... For whom? For me?"

In response, the spirit of Emily spoke with an otherworldly calmness, her voice carrying an air of solemnity. "Just now your sin is going to be ended ... the truth is going to be restored ... evil is going to be abolished. God will give to each person according to what he has done."

With solemn assurance, Emily's spirit continued, her voice carrying a weight of divine wisdom. "This judgment will not be a judgment of salvation but of one's works and rewards for these works. Salvation is by grace alone through faith alone in Jesus Christ alone. Scripture does speak about various rewards and crowns given to believers based on their service to the Lord ..."

Then, reaching out to Jesus, she gently clasped his hands in hers, her ethereal presence radiating comfort. "We'll meet in heaven. Continue to abolish evil ..."

Saying this, she and her children vanished into the ether, leaving behind a sense of peace and purpose in the courtroom.

Hearing Harris's response, his counsel tried to reassure him, saying, "Emily and her children are not here, Harris. It's just your mind playing tricks on you. Stay calm and focused. We need to prepare for the upcoming proceedings."

As the tension rose in the courtroom, Harris's counsel reassured him to maintain patience and trust in the legal process. Meanwhile, all the accused remained nervous, their eyes fixed on the floor of the accused box. The judges, under the watchful eye of policemen, reviewed the case files with grave expressions. It was a historic day for their judicial careers. Despite the tension, there was no smoking allowed, but the judges frequently requested water to quench their thirst in the intense atmosphere.

The case was presented before the bench, and after careful consideration, the honourable judges drafted the decision and affixed their signatures to it.

As they signed, the Chief Judge of the bench pronounced the decision unanimously, emphasizing that theirs was the land of Lord Gandhi, where vigilantism had no place. The strong had a duty to protect the weak.

However, while safeguarding Harris, others had inflicted immense harm upon Jesus, who stood as a beacon of truth. Therefore, the court imposed the harshest penalties on Harris and Huda …

Additionally, the court mandated the government to auction Harris's substantial assets to provide twenty lakh rupees in compensation to Jesus for the physical and mental anguish he endured.

The court also handed down severe punishments to the then Registrar, the Circle Officer, the Land Reforms Deputy Commissioner, the Chief Commissioner, the District Judge, the Superintendent of Police, and the District Magistrate under applicable sections …

Both doctors received three years of rigorous imprisonment and were fined twenty rupees each, payable as compensation to Jesus for his suffering.

Furthermore, the court granted the government the authority to auction their assets and withdraw funds from their General Provident Fund accounts to satisfy the specified compensation. Payment was mandated within seven days of the case's resolution.

All charges against Jesus were dismissed retroactively, and the sale deed registered in Harris's favour was nullified.

Any failure to implement the court's decision would result in government accountability. The decision was ratified with the court's signatures and seal.

Hearing the judgement, Harris was struck with disbelief. His demeanour suggested a man drained of vitality, as if his very essence had been engulfed by darkness.

He exclaimed, "Oh, my God. Oops … wo … ho …! I've lost everything. Once I questioned who Jesus's God was? Now I understand it all. The trial of duty's course is now complete. The answer is clear. The truth stands before us. Lies have vanished. Truth remains unhidden and untouched."

Mr End All, the defence counsel, came forward to console Harris. He advised Harris not to worry or speak out in that manner. He emphasized that they were in a court of law, not a divine court. He assured Harris that they would file an appeal the next day, presenting ample opportunity to overturn the decision. Mr End All expressed confidence, citing his extensive experience in handling murder cases where the accused were often acquitted. He assured Harris that there were certain overlooked points in their case that could potentially lead to his acquittal, and he vowed to navigate their path to victory in the apex court. Mr End All urged Harris to trust him and refrain from dwelling on any problems, assuring him that they would address all concerns in due course. Thus, he sought to console Harris and instil hope for a favourable outcome through legal proceedings.

In a state of deep distress and nervousness, Harris struggled to find the right words to respond to Mr End All's reassurances. Despite the counsel's attempts to instil hope, Harris remained gripped by the weight of his sins, feeling utterly enveloped by their darkness. He harboured a profound sense of guilt and regret for his actions, acknowledging that no one could save him now that he was consumed by the consequences of his misdeeds. Harris pleaded with the world to heed his cautionary tale, urging others not to follow the same path of ignorance and false pleasure that had led to his downfall. He expressed a deep sense of remorse, hoping that his own suffering would serve as a warning to prevent others from making the same mistakes.

Jesus couldn't contain his reaction upon hearing the judgment. The weight of the moment, the culmination of his struggle for justice, overwhelmed him, prompting an instinctive leap to his feet. His response was visceral, a physical manifestation of the emotions swirling within him – relief, vindication, and perhaps even a touch of disbelief that justice had finally been served. After enduring so much hardship and fighting against seemingly insurmountable odds, this moment of triumph filled him with an indescribable sense of elation and validation.

He said, "Hurrah! Aha! God has awarded justice to me. Truth has won. Virtue has won. Obviously, it can be said that the tears of exploitation burn not only the body of the exploiter rather also his soul. It is obvious that sins always end with decay and truth never ends. I'm going to communicate this divine message to the whole world."

He continued, "Behold, I am coming quickly, and my reward for my deed, is with me, to render to every man according to what he has done ... Then I saw a great white throne and Him who sat upon it, from whose presence earth and heaven fled away, and no place was found for them. And I saw the dead, the great and the small, standing before the throne, and books were opened; and another book was opened, which is the book of life; and the dead were judged from the things which were written in the books, according to their deeds. And the sea gave up the dead, which were in it, and death and Hades gave up the dead which were in them; and they were judged, every one of them according to their deeds."

Thus, the blessing of the law brought a victorious smile to Jesus's face – the same Jesus who was divinely empowered to achieve justice, who once lived in a state of constant suffering and sorrow. He bid farewell to all worldly miseries and sorrows. Restlessness turned into joy, and his once dim and dark face began to shine brightly. His face glowed like the North Star. He was overjoyed, smiling deeply – a smile not seen for years. The media wanted to interview him, but he stated that he had already prepared a written message for the world, which he wanted them to publish and broadcast. The media agreed and took the message. With this, he departed for Durban with a divine smile and a legal victory.

The people present were astonished when they heard the unexpected judgment. They discussed it and praised the bench that delivered the historic verdict in favour of truth, which restored faith in the judiciary and virtues. They described it as divine justice. Meanwhile, no one had any praise for Harris and the other guilty individuals. Instead, everyone commended Jesus and his self-confidence in achieving justice through honesty, despite a lifetime of suffering and losing everything except truth and virtues.

The news of this historic judgment was broadcast by local, national, and international media. It made headlines in all newspapers as well as on social and electronic media.

The next day, there was a rush among the print media to cover the news. Every daily newspaper reported the news and included Jesus's message. Even people who had never bought a newspaper in their entire lives purchased one to read about it. This led to black-marketing of the newspapers that day, with a single copy selling for twenty rupees instead of the usual four. Despite the inflated price, no newspapers were available in the market as they had all sold out before 9 a.m. Consequently, people flocked to the public library. However, it was also heavily crowded, with everyone eager to read Jesus's message. The library was packed, but unlike the market, there was no cost to read the newspapers. Every chair was occupied, and each person was allowed only one newspaper to read.

Jesus delivered a message to humanity, emphasising truth and virtues. People read it and praised him, saying that Jesus was acting under divine guidance, while Harris and the others committed their sins under the influence of malevolent forces.

Jesus's message was:

"… The journey of our soul begins when God first creates our soul. He then gives us the ability to co-create, as we can always decide what we want to experience in each of our lifetimes. As part of this project, we have a set group of issues we are required to learn about, such as trust, abandonment, abuse, judgement, control, responsibility, and love. During the journey of the soul, karma is created and karma is healed, that is just part of the adventure. This is God's way of allowing us to grow and become aware of 'who we are', to find our own place of forgiveness and unconditional love for all mankind, which then resides within us. Truth is equally valid whether anyone accepts it or not; indifferent to the special circumstances of the individual, whether he is young or old, happy or depressed; indifferent to its own relation to him, whether it benefits him or injures him, whether it restrains him from something or helps him to attain it; equally valid whether he subscribes to it with his whole heart, or professes it coldly and unemotionally, whether he lays down his life for it, or uses it merely as a means of gain; whether he himself discovered it, or he merely repeats it by rote. And only that man would have the true understanding of it, the legitimate admiration, who understands that this objectivity is the main thing, and who allows himself to be shaped in conformity with an objectivity toward that which concerns himself or some man as man."

People read this message of Jesus and praised him wholeheartedly. They felt enlightened and regarded it as a divine message. They expressed that everyone should steadfastly follow truth and virtues even in unfavourable conditions. Furthermore, they emphasized the importance of staying far away from evil.

They affirmed that Jesus possessed divine guidance, which enabled him to persist in his struggle against Harris, despite Harris's considerable influence. They acknowledged that Harris held more sway than Jesus and many others, but emphasized that truth always prevails over influence. Jesus emerged victorious because he was completely right, while Harris was entirely wrong. Inspired by Jesus's example, they resolved to follow his teachings and considered him their guide.

The Central Library in Durban was packed with a dense crowd, with barely enough room to move. People were deeply engrossed in reading the news of Jesus's victory. The library staff were overwhelmed with the influx of visitors but handled the situation with compassion, ensuring that the readers' needs were met. People found solace in satisfying their emotions through reading.

In the midst of it all, mysteriously, an elderly man appeared holding a birch leaf with a sacred message written on it in his right hand. He suddenly stood up, chanted the following verses in a melodious tone, and then vanished:

For the welfare of a good one – ruin to a wicked one –
For righteousness – age to age I am born.

.